CAR

MW01483466

Date Due

THE ELEVATOR

William Page

The Elevator: A novel by William Page
Edited and published by William Page, Lakeville, MA
Printed by BookBaby

Dedicated to my Dad, Edward

I hope you find mom in that world too.

CHAPTER 1

MY FEET ARE killing me, but I don't dare complain. I've got to keep up with the others. We've been moving at a brisk pace for some time now. Damned blisters on my feet have worn the skin bloody raw. Curse that Captain Chadwick. I was issued a brand new set of boots with my uniform before leaving England. But after reaching the colonies and settling into camp, Captain Chadwick commandeered my new boots and gave me this worn-out pair. I remember his words, "The soldier who was wearing them, didn't have a need for them anymore."

Just two months ago I was a sixteen-year-old boy from the English countryside. Today, I'm a British soldier, here in the American colonies to teach these rebels not to mess with the Crown.

We should be there soon. It was about an hour ago that the lieutenant told us to pick up the pace. He thought it best that we arrive early and set up positions. I respect Lieutenant Barnes. He's a well-trained soldier and looks after his men. He never would have treated me the way that that wretched captain did.

Lieutenant Barnes handpicked his platoon of men for this mission. The question is why did he pick me? Most of these men are battle-honed elite soldiers. I, on the other hand, am a brand new recruit. I've never even shot a man before. I suppose one needs to start somewhere. Maybe he considers this a good learning experience for me.

I remember the lieutenant saying that this mission was one of strategic importance. He mentioned that it could be a tipping point in the war. He also stated that we should be able to carry it out with very little resistance.

For now, my blisters take a back seat to my excitement as I carry up the rear of the pack. Lieutenant Barnes is up in front leading the way, followed by his most trusted soldiers. New recruits are entrusted to carry up the rear until they've proved themselves in battle. After pasting some of these colonial rebels, maybe I'll have my day up front.

Suddenly, from up ahead, I heard the sounds of men shouting as they came out of the woods. My pulse quickened, and my senses sharpened their focus. There appeared to be only six of them, and they looked to be without weapons. However, they insisted on standing their ground by blocking the road in front of us.

Our platoon came to a halt. I heard Lieutenant Barnes say, "Step aside. Get out of our way." The soldiers up front then raised their rifles, pointing to either side of the road. Keenly they watched for any movement, in the event that we had walked into a trap. Once more, the lieutenant spoke, "I will not say it again. Stand down and move aside or suffer the consequences."

The large man in front appeared to be their leader. With a deep voice, he responded, "You've reached the end of the road, Redcoat."

The soldiers up front now turned their guns away from the sides of the road and fixed their aim at these men. Lieutenant Barnes slowly and sternly said, "You men are without weapons. I will give you to the count of three to move, or we will open fire."

Their leader turned his head slightly to the left and then back to the right, looking at his men before saying, "Well, I guess it's time for us to move." That's when they boldly began to charge straight at us.

Gunfire erupted from the soldiers up front. However, those crazy rebels didn't drop. They just kept coming. As they reached the front line of soldiers, the large man punched his fist into the lieutenant's chest. He then ripped his heart out and held the still beating bloody mass up in the air like a trophy. The body of Lieutenant Barnes slammed to the ground.

For a split-second, everyone froze. One of the other rebels quickly grabbed a soldier by the head and viciously ripped it off his shoulders. A second wave of gunfire broke out from the middle of the platoon. Again, it seemed to have no effect. These crazy men were biting and tearing the limbs off the soldiers. I raised my rifle, took aim, and fired. I know I hit that man square in the chest. I saw his wound open up. Yet, he didn't seem to feel it. He just looked at me with a sinister smile. Fear ran up and down my spine. I know not what these are, but I'm getting the feeling that they're not human.

The soldier in front of me buried his sword right through that one's chest. The man-like creature backhanded the soldier to the ground. He removed the sword from his chest and impaled the soldier with it. He then came straight for me. There was no time for reloading my rifle. It didn't seem to do any damage anyway. I lunged forward with my rifle and buried the bayonet into his stomach. He looked down at it, then grabbed the rifle and snapped it in half. With his right hand he reached down and gripped my bayonet, still buried in his stomach. Showing no sign of pain, he slid the bayonet out of his stomach and slashed out at me.

I felt a biting sting at my throat. I saw blood splatter onto his face. It was my blood. I began choking and found it hard to breathe. I started to feel woozy. My head was spinning, and I collapsed to the ground. Lying there on the dirt road, I could see that the whole platoon was down. Those bloodthirsty creatures were moving about the bodies, chewing and ripping them apart.

Sadly, I rolled my watery eyes. It was then that I caught sight of her. Off to the side of the road, hiding behind the trees, there was a young girl. I wondered if she were an angel sent down for me. We locked eyes for a moment, and then I saw the fear on her face. I knew she was also in danger. *Hide. Hide yourself well,* I thought. With tears in her eyes, she slipped back behind the cover of a large tree.

It seems that I've lost all sense of feeling. My pain is gone now, and I can no longer move my body. My vision is fading into darkness, and the sounds around me are rapidly growing dim. I wish I were home.

CHAPTER 2

OVER 200 YEARS LATER

WHAT THE HELL was I thinking? I asked her out to the movies on the same night as the World Series. Brilliant move, Dawson. Damn overtime shifts, I must have got my days mixed up. This could be the night that the Sox wrap it all up. Like everyone else tonight, I should be down at the local pub with a frosty brew in hand, cheering the team on. But no, I'll be sitting in an empty movie theater munching on popcorn.

I will be with her though, and sitting in an empty movie theater with her could get interesting. I love spending time with her. She takes my mind off everything else. I even catch myself smiling the next day, replaying the moments spent with her the night before.

I continue to pace back and forth across the room with one eye on the television and the other on the clock. It's game six, top of the second, and we're losing one to nothing. A win tonight and the Sox will be World Series Champs. If they lose, it's back to Chicago for game seven.

I told her I'd pick her up at a quarter to eight. It's now seven thirty. If I catch all the stop lights green, I could be there in ten minutes...I still have some time.

Rodriguez wheels and fires a split-finger fastball, low and inside. The batter foul tips it into the catcher's mitt for strike three. He just struck out the side. This is looking good. He seems to be settling into a groove. Now, we'll be coming up to bat. But first, I think I hear nature calling.

I grabbed another Blue Moon from the fridge before drifting down the hall to the bathroom. While down the hall, I gave the mirror one last check. The moustache and beard stubble looks good, but that wavy brown hair is another story. It is sooo... frustrating, never does what I want it to. Fuck it. There's no time for fussing with it now. I have to get back to the game.

As I passed back through the kitchen, my phone began playing "Kashmir" by Led Zeppelin. Could that be her? Maybe she was running late. Yeah...That would mean more game time for me. Drawing the phone from my pocket, I saw that the call was from an old friend of mine, John Thompson. It's been a while since I last saw him. I pulled back a chair and sat down at the kitchen table.

"Hey, J.T.. What's up?"

"Dawson, whatcha up to? Come on over and watch the game. Frankie, Gomes, and the rest of the boys are coming over. It'll be like old times. I got a cooler of beer, pizzas, and a bottle of Crown Royal. We'll get a card game going."

"Sorry, J.T., too short notice. I got a date tonight."

"Yeah, it was kinda spur of the moment. Hey, bring her over too. We'll teach her how to play cards. Come on, for old times' sake."

I burst out in laughter back at him. "No way, J.T.. Once you guys get drunk, you'll start feeding her stories about me and old girl-friends. And that's only the beginning. Then you'll all be laughing under your breath as you begin to fabricate tales of me and other girlfriends, which I never really had, just to see how wild a story you can get her to believe. By the end of the night she'll be looking at me like she doesn't know me." I laughed again as this scenario played out in my mind. "Ohh...Yeah. You guys will have her thinking I'm wanted in three states, been married twice, and have four kids already, one with the Governor's daughter."

"Oh...You bastard," J.T. laughed back, in his big hearty voice. "I thought it was four states. Alright, Dawson, we'll drink the first shot of Crown to you. Have a good time. Don't do anything I wouldn't do."

"Good to hear from ya, J.T.. Say hey to the guys for me."

"Will do, Dawson."

On returning to the living room, I find that the Sox have a man on second base with no outs. This could be the inning. I slowly sank into the sofa thinking, *I'll just watch a couple more batters.*

Forty minutes later, I grabbed my leather jacket and out the door I went, cursing at every red light on the way.

I then remembered the phone call from J.T.. A huge grin came over my face, and I started laughing on the inside. A card game meant coolers of beer, cans of nuts, pizzas, and bottles of whiskey or Sambuca for drinking shots. We'd play cards and tell jokes all night. The ballgame would be on, but we'd only catch the replays when something exciting happened. Shots would be drank to homeruns, great catches, ass-kicking card hands, along with great bluffs, and to any pretty girl we saw that day. By four o'clock in the morning no one would remember who won the ballgame, whose turn it was, or even who dealt. That was the past and those were good times, but now I'm headed down a different road.

My name is William Dawson. But, everyone calls me by my last name, Dawson. I'm a rookie cop in a small town outside of Boston. My girl is a beautiful, fiery, Sicilian, named Sophia Montelini. Sophia is a beautiful name, and that's what everyone calls her. Everyone, that is, except me. I like to call her Sophie.

We met last year when I was shopping for a Christmas gift for my dad. He's a bow hunter and shops for all his gear at a little archery store in the next town over. My dad frequently described the store's owner as a sort of eccentric man with long hair, a beard, and a disheveled appearance.

I still remember that day. As I walked through the front door my jaw dropped open with a sense of awe at the sight of all the extraordinary hunting and target gear on display. While strolling through the store aisles, musing at the items, a girl walked up beside me and asked, "Can I help you?" I turned to look at her and found myself spellbound. I just stared at her, dumbstruck.

Once again she asked, "Can I help you find anything?"

After blinking my eyes a few times, I regained control of my senses. "Sorry," I replied. "You kinda caught me off guard. I was more expecting the mountain man type. You know, a scruffy guy with a beard, who looks like he just crawled out of the woods." I then thought, *Did I just say that? Come on, Dawson. Take your boot out of your mouth.*

She teased, "Well, he's out back. I can go get him for you if you'd like."

"No…No… I'd much rather be waited on by you," I quickly answered.

Her eyes took on a warm glow, and a playful smile came to her face. I told her I was looking to buy a new bow, as a Christmas gift for my dad. I mentioned to her that my dad, oftentimes, was not an easy person to buy for, and that my knowledge of bows was minimal. I asked her whether my purchase was exchangeable in the event that he wasn't satisfied.

"Absolutely," she reassured.

I still remember following Sophie down the store aisle to the bow section. There was something about the way she walked. I couldn't take my eyes off her.

She selected and demonstrated numerous compound bows for me, explaining the differences and dynamics of how each one worked. I paid very close attention to her, while hearing absolutely nothing. She then left me to ponder my decision, as she returned back up front to the cash register.

There are times when too many choices leave you wrestling with indecisiveness. It took me a while as I slowly scrutinized the wide selection of bows for the one I felt my dad would be the most comfortable with. Finally, satisfied with my choice, I made my way back up front to the pretty girl at the checkout.

Sophie smiled at me as she saw me approach. With a soft playful voice she asked, "Did you find everything you were looking for?"

Looking deep into her eyes, I replied, "Yes…Right at the register." That was eleven months ago.

CHAPTER 3

I PULLED MY truck into the driveway of the little, white, cape-style house. Sophie lived there all year round. Her mom and dad own the house, but were only there during the summer months. They preferred to spend the rest of the year living at their other home in Florida. Sophie and Jack had the whole house to themselves. Jack's a bit of a psycho, and he definitely has some anger management issues. But, he's also a pussy. That's right, Jack's a purebred Norwegian Forest cat, whatever the hell that is. Personally, I think they should have left him in the forest.

There's never a dull moment when Jack and I get together. He loves pouncing on me and sinking his claws in. I, in turn, enjoy antagonizing him. I try to see how fast I can get him to swat those paws without catching me.

Jack and I usually just eyeball each other if Sophie is in the room. With cats it's hard to tell, but I often think he's giving me dirty looks. I like to throw some back in his direction just for good measure. It keeps him in the game. Once she leaves the room, that's when Jack gets up and picks his angle to pounce.

Yeah...Jack knows how to keep the scold-factor down. He's a master of the hit and run. Then he sits there looking all innocent, as if, *Who? Me? I don't know what this guy's talking about.* When I first told her about this, Sophie didn't believe me. She had to hide behind the door casing to see it for herself.

I told Sophie, "I think he's jealous, and he's trying to tell me to leave."

I remember she smiled back at me saying, "Maybe he's trying to tell you that the pretty girl just left the room, and you should go after her."

As I got out of the truck my eyes were drawn to the lamp post by a busy throng of little white moths. They were doing their nightly dance, fluttering about the warm light, casting fleeting shadows off the house and walkway. Seeing the post light still on was actually a positive sign. However, I didn't doubt that there was a pretty good chance she would be angry. Quietly, I strolled up onto the porch to ring the doorbell.

She must have been waiting by the door. I say this because I was still pressing the doorbell as the door whooshed open. There she stood with fire in her eyes. "You're late, Dawson. The movie already started." She was wearing that angry face and beating me down with her eyebrows.

"Sorry, babe. Whoa...You really outdid yourself tonight. You look stunning." I stepped in while admiring her glossy dark brown hair, done up in big curls, flowing down past her shoulders. Sophie's skin was smooth and olive toned. Her big, soft, brown eyes always seemed to tug at me. She was wearing black jeans, showing off her long legs and that cute little bum. I could see in her face that she enjoyed how I was looking at her. However, she still didn't want to let go of that other matter. The one that got her angry in the first place. For the moment, I remained mesmerized by the view.

My thoughts were then shaken loose by Sophie's voice. "Dawson, it's nine o'clock. Where the hell have ya been?"

For lack of a better excuse, I replied, "Sorry, babe. I was watching the World Series and lost track of time."

She gave me a stern, puzzled look for a few seconds before scolding, "You are sooo... in the doghouse." As she continued to stare at me her expression softened, as well as her tone. "But, at least you didn't lie to me and fabricate some wild story. We can still head down to the movie theater and hang out until the next show. I just need a moment to do my eyelashes before I grab my coat," she said as she left the kitchen.

I knew she wasn't ready.

From the bathroom I heard Sophie call out, "You're not going to believe it Dawson, but I had that same dream again last night."

She keeps having this haunting dream about aliens invading our planet. I teased, "Yeah, well, I did some research on this subject and I'm afraid there's no hope for you, Sophie. It's only a matter of time before they drag you off to an asylum."

Sophie leaned her head thru the doorway with a smirking tongue-in-cheek face. She playfully scolded, "You're not much help, Dawson."

"Sorry, sweetie!" I laughed. She then retreated back to the bathroom.

As I turned toward the refrigerator I spotted Jack perched up on top peering down at me. That little furball was just waiting for me to open the door so he could pounce down on me. I snarled at him and flipped him the bird. He gave me a quick upward flick with his paw, then pulled it back and started licking it, all the while, never taking his eyes off me. The two of us innocently dropped the confrontation when Sophie re-entered the room. However, as Sophie and I headed for the door, Jack jumped down to the countertop and gave the back of my arm a slap with his paw. It brought a smirk to my face. In return, I looked back over my shoulder and gave him a sarcastic sneer.

Once the two of us were out on the porch, Sophie asked, "Do you want to take my car?"

"Nope. We'll take my truck."

"How come you never want to take my car? You know I'll let you drive."

We climbed into the truck. Sophie scooched over next to me on the seat. I turned to her, saying, "This is why I wanted to take the truck. When you sit this close..." I paused and brought my hand to my chest. "I get a warm, tingling feeling in here."

With raised eyebrows and parted lips, Sophie's eyes took on a glow. She leaned over, kissed my cheek, and whispered in my ear, "I love you, Dawson."

"Sooo... Does this mean that I'm out of the doghouse?"

With a smirk on her face she replied, "Not on your life."

I pressed my tongue against my cheek to keep from laughing while I turned the key. The truck fired right up and Zeppelin's "Over The Hills And Far Away" began to pour out of the speakers.

Sophie immediately went for the CD case. "Dawson, didn't I leave my Motown CD in your truck?"

"Yup. It's in there." I knew where she was going with this. I also knew it would take her a while to find it. That's because I had tucked it in behind one of the other discs.

As she thumbed through my CD case she said, "Dawson, you do realize there's more to the music world than just Led Zeppelin and Pink Floyd?"

"Yes, dear," I playfully mocked.

Sophie bit her bottom lip with a smile and gave me a playful eye as she slid the Motown CD into the player. The Temptation's "Ain't Too Proud To Beg" began to flow from the speakers. I have to give credit to Sophie. She was really good at choosing the right music to set a mood.

The movie theater was on the other side of town. It was a large complex with three floors and twelve screens. After wading through the ticket line, we found that we still had forty-five minutes to kill. So, with a soda and a bag of popcorn in hand, we found our way to an empty bench near the rear of the lobby.

There we sat, watching the people filter in. Over to our left there were two elevators, and in front of us stood a wide stairway. We played a game of trying to guess which people would wait in line for an elevator and which would use the stairway. While playing this game I happened to glance over my shoulder to the right, and noticed a third elevator, slightly behind us. "Hey, Sophie. I don't remember there being another elevator over on that wall. Do you?"

Sophie gave me a sassy, flirtatious look. Then with a sarcastic tone, she replied, "No. But, we're always late and in a rush. We probably never had time to notice."

She was being cutesy, throwing a verbal dart at me for our being late. Really...Does she know how long it takes her to get ready? That's the reason we're usually late. I know. I have the claw marks to prove it.

Anyway...I wondered why, with the lines at the other elevators, no one used this one? I got up and strolled over to check it out. To the side of the door was a little metal plaque with the words *out of service* glowing from it. Below the plaque was a single call button. I pressed the button, and the elevator door slid open. The floor of the elevator was covered with a bright carpet of red. As I leaned in, I noticed that the entire wall to my left was a mirror. The other walls appeared to be made of stainless steel. I stepped in and turned to Sophie, waving at her to follow.

She slowly moved her head from side to side and mouthed, "No way."

"But, I want to kiss you," I pleaded.

"You can kiss me right out here, in the lobby."

"Not the way I want to kiss you."

A devilish grin came over her face. She set the bag of popcorn down, then scampered over and in. The elevator door immediately closed behind her. Sophie became worried. "What if we get stuck in here?"

"We call 911. They come and get us out. There's nothing to worry about."

Glancing toward the mirror, I teased, "Whoa...That's one hot looking girl over there. How come you're not getting mad at me for looking at her?"

"The only reason I'm going to get mad is because you haven't kissed her yet," she playfully hinted. To this I laughed, and then leaned toward the mirror, kissing the reflection of her lips. With a sarcastic smile Sophie looked at my reflection in the mirror and teased, "Did you enjoy that, Dawson?"

"No. It was cold and hard, nothing like the soft, warm, wetness of the real thing." I started toward Sophie. But as I did, the elevator shifted slightly, throwing us off balance. This was followed by the feeling of tremors coming through the floor of the elevator. They were mild and rhythmic, about three to five seconds apart, coinciding with the distant sound of heavy metal clunking. "Did you touch any buttons?" I asked.

"No," she winced, as she threw her body against mine, clinging with both hands. It was then that I noticed there were no buttons on the wall to push, not even one to open the door.

16

CHAPTER 4

IN THE MOMENTS that followed, the magnitude of the tremors and heavy clunking grew more intense. Sophie was still clinging tightly to me, and I could sense her fear growing. I have to confess that I was a bit nervous too, but did my best not to show it. That would only serve to escalate her fears. Instead, I tried to remain calm and vigilant, waiting to see what was about to unfold.

Suddenly, we heard a crumpling metal sound. The elevator then rocked and shook as if it were being ripped out of the wall structure it was housed in. Whatever was happening, it was swift, and over in a matter of seconds. This was followed by a few minutes of nothing but an eerie silence. It was as if we were floating in a dead stillness.

Quietly, we began to move, however, not in the usual way. There wasn't that upward pull or downward drop feeling that is typical with an elevator. Instead, it felt as if we were traveling sideways with incredible speed. At times, I felt a slight pitch to the left or right as if we were changing direction. Eventually, everything eased to a stop.

We sat for a moment in total silence. Finally, the elevator door slowly slid open. Bright sunlight poured in upon us forcing my eyes to squint with a dull ache until they adjusted. When we entered the movie complex, the moon and stars were in full bloom. But now, the sun was out, in all its glory. It was the middle of the day. There was no movie theater, no cars, or even a parking lot. We were sitting in a small grassy meadow surrounded by a forest of trees. Just beyond this grassy area I could see a small, narrow dirt road that wandered through the forest. Sophie and I looked at each other confused. Needless to say, we weren't in any great hurry to venture one step outside of the door.

All of a sudden the mirrored wall of the elevator began to twinkle with hundreds of little starry lights. They danced and floated across the surface of the mirror, eventually gelling together to form a message.

He has my key
Bestowed by the Watcher
Take it away from him
It's your only hope for return
The bag outside will profit you

Once read, the words faded from view leaving the two of us looking at our bewildered reflections in the mirror. With no other choice, we stepped out of the elevator. I noticed a brown backpack lying in the grass to our right. The elevator door quickly closed behind us, and the sound of rumbling machinery started again.

Frustrated, Sophie began pounding her fist on the door of the elevator. I wrapped my arm around her waist and quickly pulled her back as the ground started shaking. The entire elevator slowly began turning around. As it did, it screwed itself down into the ground. Instantly, the grass began to repair itself, to appear as if it hadn't been disturbed at all.

A look of distress came over Sophie's face. Her eyes narrowed, her lower lip pushed upward, and the sides of her mouth turned down. "That thing just disappeared into the ground. How the hell are we going to get out of here?"

I checked my phone – no service. With not much else to offer, I replied, "Like the message said, we just have to find this man and take the elevator key from him."

"We don't know where the hell we are, and we don't have a clue who this guy is." Sophie then threw her hands up in the air. "Why on earth, do I listen to you, Dawson?"

It was pretty obvious that her distress was festering. I tried to redirect her before she entered total meltdown mode. "Because you trust me. I'm clever, confident, and good at problem solving." I calmly replied. This did nothing to improve the situation. She was frantic and losing control.

Sophie started walking in a circle, talking rapidly while waving her arms up and down. "We just fell down the rabbit hole, or landed in Oz, or some other dimension..."

I cut her short. "Sophia, get a grip!" This brought her back down to earth, while also getting her really pissed off.

Sophie's eyes pierced me like daggers. "Don't...tell me to get a grip!" she snapped with an irascible tone.

"Okay. Okay. Wrong choice of words. Let's just try to hold this together. We're not injured. We're okay. We're with each other, and we have a loose sense of what we need to do."

Just then, off to our left, we heard a horse drawn carriage approaching along the little dirt road. As it drew closer, the driver took notice of us in the grassy clearing and pulled the carriage to a stop. It was a strange sight, this old-fashioned coach, but then again so was everything else around us. The carriage was black and completely enclosed with a roof and doors. It had four large wooden spoke wheels, a luggage rack in back, and a small lantern mounted on the side. A metal step hung down below the door for ease of access. The driver sat high up in front on a cushioned bench seat, complete with a foot rest and splash shield. In front of him, a handsome chestnut colored stallion provided all the muscle that was needed.

The driver tied off the reins before slowly making his way down from his perch. He was a tall, slim man, who sported an old-fashioned wool suit along with a scally cap. He had dark eyes, black wavy hair with long sideburns, and a waxed mustache. For a moment, he just stood there staring at us with a deadpan face. Then, after removing his hat, he gave a nod with his head toward the carriage door.

I picked up the backpack and walked past Sophie, saying, "Someone knows we've arrived. Come on, Cinderella, or we're gonna miss the ball." I could hear her grumbling a few choice adjectives under her breath as she followed me to the carriage door.

As the driver opened the carriage door for us I turned to him and asked, "Not that it matters, but where might our destination be?" He said nothing, glaring back at me with those dark empty eyes and that vacant expression. Once again, he nodded his head toward the carriage for me to get in.

This didn't sit well with Sophie. She pushed me aside and waved her index finger in front of his face. "Listen you. I'm not getting into this carriage until you tell us where you're taking us."

In a slow, dull monotone, he responded, "That would be Graveswood Manor, My Lady."

Sophie angrily blurted out, "Fine," then began climbing up into the carriage. As she did, I gave her cute little bum a pinch. She winced as she sat down on the seat, glaring at me.

I leaned in with an innocent face, saying, "Just testing to make sure we're not in a dream." She scowled back at me. I tossed the backpack in on the floor of the carriage before climbing up and in. The driver latched the door behind me. He then ascended to his seat, up high in front. With a snap of the reins we were off, and on our way.

Inside the carriage there were two, soft and plush, gray velvet seats that faced each other. The walls and ceiling were also covered with a gray velvet material. Sophie and I sat in the rear seat, facing forward.

"At least he spoke to you," I said, before adding with a chuckle, "My Lady."

"Yeah. What was that all about?"

"You should have kept him talking. I wonder what this Graveswood Manor is?"

"He creeped me out with that stern face and those dark hollow eyes. I had to turn away."

"Yeah. I know what you mean. There is a cold emptiness about him," I said. Sophie slid up against me, tucking her arm under mine and laying her head against my shoulder. My hand slipped in and came to rest between her thighs. I kept one eye out the window to take note of any turns or landmarks. I wanted to be sure that we could find our way back, when the time comes. But, all I saw along the way were trees and fields of grass.

CHAPTER 5

As THE CARRIAGE strolled down this narrow dirt road I noticed it seemed to instill a feeling of romance. The carriage gently rocked and swayed you as it traveled along. Cool, brisk, country fresh air sifted through the windows while you listened to the sound of the wagon wheels and the click-clack of the horse's hooves. The rustic nature of the ride, with all its simple elegance, seemed to bring you back to a time long ago, and warmed you inside.

Sophie whispered to me, "Do you think he's the guy with the key?"

"No. I think the holder of the key knows we've arrived and has sent out this minion to pick us up."

"But arrived where, Dawson? Where do you think we are?"

"Not sure. I'm still confused. And I forgot what the message from the elevator said. Do you remember?" Of course, I knew she'd remember. She had the mind of an elephant, never forgetting, always filing, sorting, and tucking everything away.

"You forgot already," she said, trying to hold back the laughter. She couldn't resist teasing, "Must be all the drugs and alcohol you did in your younger days, huh?"

"Hey...Hey," I protested.

Sophie giggled, "What would you do without me, Dawson?"

"Alright. Don't let it go to your head. Come on. Refresh my memory."

"It said: *He has my key, bestowed by the Watcher. Take it away from him. It's your only hope for return.*"

"I was afraid of that. Sophie, have you noticed the condition of this carriage? Either it's had a meticulous restoration, or it's actually still new. Couple that with the driver's grooming, his attire, and this narrow dirt road. A while ago you posed the question, 'Where are we?' I'm more inclined to ask when? If the elevator had transported us somewhere else on earth, we wouldn't need its key to get back home. However, if it transported us to another place in time..."

"You think we've gone back in time?"

"It seems that way to me. But, I don't understand the line about the Watcher."

Sophie sat up quickly. "And what's in the bag? We forgot all about the bag. Profit us...Is it money?"

I reached down, scooped up the backpack, and gently placed it on the seat in front of us. Turning to Sophie, I noticed her face was lit up with anticipation. I teased, "You look like a kid on Christmas morning."

"Come on, Dawson. Don't make me wait."

"Alright," I laughed. I slowly slid the zipper across and pulled the sides open. On top there were two pistols. I reached in and pulled them out, one in each hand. Glancing back at Sophie, I saw her wide-eyed with her mouth hanging open. This was definitely not what she had expected. In a slow quiet voice, I said, "It appears as though there's going to be some obstacles along the way. Someone must be standing between us and that key. It seems we may have to take it by force."

Sophie's face wore a pouty expression. She said, "I thought there would be gems or money in there. Instead, we got guns."

I looked into her eyes and whispered, "I need you to be strong. Things may get ugly, a bit bloody, and quite scary. You have to be able to pull that trigger."

"I can shoot. I just never shot anyone before."

"Neither have I," I said.

Placing the pistols on the seat, I reached back into the bag and pulled out the next item. It was about fourteen to sixteen inches long with a hand grip at its midsection. There were multiple pulleys and cables that ran along its length. I stared at it with a puzzled look, saying, "I have no idea what this is."

"I do," Sophie piped in, full of excitement. She took it from my hand, examining it closely. "I've heard of these, but never actually saw one before." She wrapped her hand around the grip. Then, holding it out at arm's length, she pressed a button. I heard two clicks. Instantly, from each end of the main body, out sprang another shaft about a foot long. Each spring loaded shaft carried the pulleys and cables out along with it.

Sophie was beaming with contentment. "It's a retractable compound bow. Press one button and it springs out to three times its

length. Press another button and it retracts to compact carry size."
She held the bow out at arm's length, drawing the bowstring back to
her face to get a feel for the bow.

"That's pretty cool. Now you look like a kid who just got the
best Christmas gift they ever could have wished for."

Without moving her head, she shifted her eyes toward me with
a smile and said, "Better."

I reached back into the bag and pulled out a quiver filled with
arrows. Sophie drew an arrow out of the quiver. "High quality carbon
fiber," she declared as her gaze slid from the tail feathers to the tip of
the arrow. Sophie then stopped for a moment as she scrutinized the
tip of the arrow. "Dawson, these arrowheads are made of silver."

She was staring at me now with a sense of urgency. I picked
up one of the pistols and kicked out the magazine to examine the
ammo. "The bullets are also made of silver," I replied.

We were looking at each other with mouths wide open, unable
to talk. I could feel a shiver running up and down my spine. By the
look on her face, I'd say she felt the same. I threw my hand back into
the bag and came out with two scarfs, both silver in color with a texture that felt like satin.

Sophie began to examine one of the scarfs. "It's amazing. This
feels and moves like satin, but it's made of metal – real silver. This
is right out of the future. How can it be so pliable and still keep its
strength?" She continued to flex and poke the satiny metal material.

I noticed a note attached to the second scarf. I took it off
and read it out loud. "*You won't be totally safe, but these are a good
deterrent. Keep them around your neck at all times between dusk and
dawn.*"

The two of us sat motionless, peering straight ahead. Simultaneously, we murmured, "Vampires."

"Dawson, maybe you should pinch me again. This just gets stranger by the minute. What else is in that bag?"

I reached in and came out with a sword, sheathed in a scabbard. I slowly drew the sword out, revealing a double-edged silver broadsword with a two prong hilt. It was short, about thirty inches from end to end, but it had good balance and a comfortable hand grip. The shorter length actually appealed to me. It would be easier to carry and more maneuverable in close quarters.

"Have you ever used a sword before?" Sophie asked.

"Yeah. I've used both a Katana and broadsword in my martial arts training. I'm pretty comfortable with a broadsword. But, I'm not going to kid myself. I am by no means an accomplished swordsman."

Other than these items, the bag held pistol holsters, extra magazines and ammo, along with a couple of Velcro harnesses. One harness was for the retractable crossbow. It provided three options for carrying the weapon. The crossbow could be worn along the outside of the thigh, diagonally across the chest, or at the waist. The other harness was for the broadsword. It provided for the sword to be carried across one's back, either diagonally or vertically.

CHAPTER 6

FOR THE MOMENT Sophie seemed preoccupied with her new toy. She was getting familiar with how it snapped in and out of the clip on the harness. She kept playing with the buttons, making the bow extend and retract. She also practiced her aim out the window at some of the trees passing by. While watching her I thought, *This is good. Get comfortable with it. Make it second nature. Then, when the time comes, you won't have to think about it.* I quietly left her to her amusement while I stared out the window next to me trying to make sense out of what had happened to us. I also began to ponder what lies ahead. If we get caught up in violent encounters, I'm not quite sure how Sophie will react.

There are, however, two things I do know. First, and foremost, I need to keep her out of harm's way. Secondly, I need to keep my edge and remain dauntless. If I were to show any sign of fear, Sophie might think all is lost and begin to come apart at the seams. There's no way I can let that happen. Bold and confident is how I need to approach what lies ahead. In turn, maybe some of that might rub off on her.

A minute or two later, I heard Sophie say, "Dawson, what's next? What do we do now?"

I turned to her and looked into those deep brown eyes, thinking...*She's so damn alluring.* I quietly answered, "Someone is on our side, loading us up with all this weaponry that plays into our strengths."

"Who do you think it is?"

I shrugged my shoulders, saying, "I don't know. But, I have a feeling that things are going to get violent and bloody. Are you going to be okay?"

"Dawson, I'll have no problems letting the arrows fly. I can hold my own. You just make sure that you can keep up with me."

A tongue-in-cheek smile came over my face. I couldn't believe this was coming out of her mouth, but I was liking it. Put a bow in this girl's hand and she finds a world of confidence. This appeared to be a good sign. I only hoped that she wouldn't buckle under pressure. "Remember, Sophie. When in battle it's either us or them. Don't give them an inch. Get angry, keep your edge, and take them down quickly."

Since it was still daytime, we agreed to put all the other items back into the bag and just carry the pistols under our coats. When sunset approached we would fully gear up. The two of us would also try to stay together at all times and avoid getting separated. Whatever we were facing, we would need to be as prepared as possible.

Out of the window to my right, I noticed we were coming up to a clearing with a large wrought iron fence separating someone's property line from the road. I leaned closer to the window to get a better view of what was up ahead. We were approaching a huge old mansion. Behind it I could see a barn along with some lesser cabins and sheds. The mansion had a dull, gray, weathered appearance. I surmised it was made out of stone or cement. It was set back about four hundred feet from the road. There was a large circular driveway in front of the house that trailed back toward the main road, passing between two huge willow trees along the way. Across the front of the mansion a large sitting-porch stretched from one side to the other. At its center a wide stairway reached down to the driveway. The house had very tall windows, leading me to believe that the rooms inside must have high ceilings. I also assumed from the pattern of their layout that this house had three floors.

The carriage slowed down and turned into the driveway through two open iron gates. Hanging on the fence next to the entrance was an old, weather-tarnished sign. As we passed by it, I read the words Graveswood Manor.

CHAPTER 7

As THE HORSE brought us up the driveway between the two huge willow trees, I began to wonder if we would find our host here to be a friend or foe. The driver eased the coach to a stop in front of the stairway to the front porch. Up on the porch to the left I saw two rocking chairs, while far over to the right sat a wicker fan-back chair and loveseat.

Immediately, the front door opened and a short round man came down the steps to greet us. I would guess him to be in his mid-forties. His hair, a mix of reddish brown and gray was short, curly, and quite receded. He wore wire-rimmed reading spectacles that hung low on his nose. As he walked toward us it was quite evident that he had a noticeable hitch in his gait.

"Welcome travelers. Welcome to Graveswood. My name is Isaac. Come...I will assist you." Sophie and I began to climb down from the carriage. "Please sir. Allow me to carry your baggage for you."

"No. That won't be necessary. I'll carry it," I replied, slinging the bag over my shoulder.

Isaac looked up at the driver and barked, "Malcolm, put the coach away. Be sure to feed and groom the horse. In the meantime, I shall show our guests around."

Malcolm grunted something under his breath back at Isaac before giving the reins a snap. Quickly, the horse started on its way, back to the barn. Isaac stood watching the carriage as it turned and moved past the corner of the house. He then said, "Follow me," as he began walking back down the driveway toward the road.

Sophie and I looked at each other puzzled, expecting to go up the stairs and into the house. Isaac, already about twenty feet ahead of us, stopped and looked back, saying, "Come...This way...Hurry."

I understood the expression on Sophie's face to say, *He's not right of mind.* I grinned back at her while shrugging my shoulders. We then proceeded to follow him down the drive. His pace was brisk, but with those short legs and that hitch in his walk, we caught up quickly.

"You are not safe here. It would be like entering a lion's den. Thank God, you came at this time." Isaac kept turning and looking back over his shoulder as we went. He was panting as he spoke. I wasn't sure if this was due to nervousness or his lack of physical conditioning.

"Turn right at the gate and continue down the road about one mile to the village. I know you have many questions. No one will answer them. Everyone is afraid to talk. Once in the village, seek out the old woman, Isabelle. She knows more than anyone else and does not fear them."

"Who lives here?" I asked.

"Voltaire."

"Is he a vampire?"

Isaac, with a fearful look on his face, nodded his head a number of times.

"You said them. Are there other vampires?" I asked.

Isaac continued nodding his head with the same worried look. "Once you reach the village, find Isabelle and do as she says." Isaac cupped his hands together and looked to the sky. "I pray that she will assist you."

As we approached the front gate, Isaac stopped to say, "Please, besides Isabelle, tell no one that I helped you get away. I was merely showing you around, and the two of you escaped."

I nodded, saying, "I understand. Thank you, Isaac. We appreciate the help."

"Godspeed to both of you," he said, as he turned and scurried back toward the mansion. We took Isaac's advice, bypassing the mansion for now and continuing along the dirt road in search of the village.

CHAPTER 8

"Now, I've heard of godfather, godmother, God-given, and God-forsaken. But, what the hell is Godspeed?" Sophie asked.

I laughed at her tone and how fast she blurted that out. Turning my head to her with a smirk, I said, "Godspeed means good fortune on your journey."

"Well...Let's hope he's right. He seemed like a pretty nervous guy, that Isaac. What do you make of him?"

I turned and looked behind us at the gloomy mansion, saying, "That place has trouble written all over it. Isaac took a big risk in steering us away from there. I'm not sure why he did it. But, he appears to be on our side. That's enough for me to like him already."

"He seems to have a lot of faith in Isabelle. I hope she will be of some help to us," Sophie replied.

"Whatever she can tell us about them will be a plus. The more we know about our enemy, the better off we'll be while walking into his camp."

"Dawson, why does the road have this hump running down the middle of it?"

"You are a city girl, Sophie. It's called the crown of the road. Wagons with heavy loads pass through here never touching the middle. Their wheels wear down these paths on either side. The only thing that rides the middle would be a lone horse pulling a wagon."

"How do you know about all this stuff?

"I'm just a wealth of information," I teased.

"Oh, pl..ease! I should have worn my boots."

In no time at all we found ourselves coming up on a small village. It looked as if it had been carved right out of the old west. All the structures were crafted out of rough pine boards. There was a tavern, a boarding house, a supply store, and a livery area with stables. A number of little houses and cabins were also scattered about. In the center of the village there was an old well, made of stone. Hanging above it was a water bucket and rope, wrapped around a roller that turned by a big crank handle attached on one side.

We noticed a man who was coming out of the supply store and approached him. As we drew near he seemed to become a bit nervous and apprehensive. "Excuse me. Do you know where we might find Isabelle?" I asked. The man stared at us for what seemed like more than a moment. I began to wonder if he was Malcolm's brother. So little expression, so few words. "The old woman named Isabelle?" I asked again.

After creepily staring for a few more seconds, he pointed across the way, saying, "That house over there, next to the stables." He then abruptly turned around and walked back into the store.

While crossing the center of the village, Sophie asked, "Do we really look that strange?"

Being a smartass, I said, "Speak for yourself. I fit right in."

She laughed back at me, "Yeah, that's what's scary." I squinted my eyes and growled at her, knowing I had walked right into that one.

When we arrived at the front door of the little house I reached up with my fist to give it a knock, only to notice that the door was already slowly starting to open. I stopped my fist in mid-air and drew it back. With a grin, I looked at Sophie and teased, "Must be a girl thing." She answered with a quick elbow to my ribs.

The door hinges creaked and moaned as the door slowly opened the rest of the way to reveal a woman much younger than I expected, middle forties to fifty at best. Could this possibly be Isabelle? Isaac had referred to her as an old woman. I'd be hard pressed to say that. She had shoulder length medium brown hair with just a touch of gray. The woman was thin and actually quite shapely. Time had been kind to her. Her skin was tanned and smooth, with the exception of a few telltale wrinkles around her eyes, which resembled the same shade of blue as mine. There was no doubt that she must have been a very beautiful young woman, for she was still quite attractive now. She stood looking at us, as we did her, for a moment or two.

"Isabelle?" I asked.

"Yes, Dawson. You and Sophia, please come in," she replied.

Sophie and I just froze, looking at each other. We hadn't told anyone our names. How did she know?

"I baked some bread," Isabelle said with a comforting voice. "We'll have soup and bread. Come on in and sit with me."

I looked at Sophie with a grin, then nodded my head toward the doorway, saying, "My Lady." She gave me that raised eyebrow look that seemed to suggest, *Do you have to act crazy right now?* She proceeded to step through the doorway. As I followed her in, I whispered over her shoulder, "Say, if I refer to you as My Lady, does that mean that you have to refer to me as My Lord?"

She quickly whispered back from the side of her mouth, "Yeah, that's not gonna happen." With a quiet chuckle, I closed the door behind me.

Immediately, my senses were teased by the aroma of freshly baked bread. As I turned from the door I saw that we were in the main room of Isabelle's cottage. It was a large country kitchen. In the center of the room stood a round wooden table with four chairs. Behind it, a fire was burning in a huge stone fireplace with an opening that was at least four feet high. A cast iron pot hung from a hinged metal arm that could swing into or out of the fireplace. Off to the left and right of the fireplace were doors that led back to other rooms. Along one wall of the kitchen there was a counter top with shelves up above it. These shelves were filled with containers of numerous herbs and spices.

Isabelle proceeded to hand me a small wooden paddle. I'm not going to say where my mind started to go with that, but I glanced at Sophie with a devilish grin and raised an eyebrow. Sophie's eyes opened wide, then she proceeded to scold me with a frown. Isabelle tapped me on the arm while pointing to a small arched opening with a tin door built into the stone face of the fireplace. She asked if I could bring from it, the loaf of bread to the table.

Meanwhile, Isabelle had Sophie hold the bowls for her as she carefully dipped the ladle into the pot and filled each of them with hot soup. I slid the paddle under the loaf of bread and carefully removed it from the oven. Slowly, I carried it over and placed it at the center of the table. Isabelle sat down at the table with her back to the fireplace. Sophie and I sat across from Isabelle, with a full view of her and the fire slowly dancing in the background. Sophie and I knew enough not to overstep our boundaries and begin firing questions at Isabelle. It seemed only proper for us to bide our time and allow her to initiate the conversation.

Isabelle was in no hurry. She slowly sliced off bread for the three of us before we began our meal. I think it was her intention to eat first and talk later. I'm sure Sophie found this a bit frustrating. I, on the other hand, was hungry and had no problem with it.

The soup was a hearty blend of beef and vegetables, with subtle hints of added herbs and spices. The soft, warm, oven baked bread melted in my mouth. Isabelle must have known all along that this combination of a warm fire and savory food would ease the two of us into a more relaxed and comfortable mood.

CHAPTER 9

ONCE SHE HAD finished her soup, Isabelle raised her head and looked across at us. Softly, slowly, and with an air of equanimity she began to speak. "People around here are fearful. They don't talk much and spend their nights quietly hiding. I know you have many questions, to which I believe I have the answers you seek. But, if I am to help you, I need to know how sincere you are. I will ask each of you something, to which you must respond truthfully if you wish to gain my assistance. I will know if your answers are genuine."

Isabelle's gaze turned toward Sophie. "I would like you, Sophia, to tell me of a recent romantic event that will remain forever special in your memory."

Sophie timidly gazed down at her soup for a second. Bashful and embarrassed, she slowly lifted her head. "Well, last week Dawson and I took a ride down to the oceanfront to watch the waves roll in. We were sitting in Dawson's pickup truck, gazing out at the moon and stars across the water. From across the bay, Minot's Ledge

Lighthouse endlessly spelled out 'I - love - you.' The tide was high, and about every ten seconds another wave would come rolling in, its surf breaking against the beach and then slowly retreating away. There's something about the sound of the surf as it crashes in and then slowly slides back out that is both relaxing and seductive. One thing led to another, and the clothes began to come off. We made love right there on the seat of his pickup truck. It wasn't long before the windows steamed up, and we became drenched in a passionate sweat. I remember afterwards, he held me tight and I could feel his heart beating right through my breast. He, in turn, could feel my heart beating against his chest. We held each other close, laughing with amusement. It was a warm and special moment."

Isabelle smiled from ear to ear and said, "Thank you, my dear. You are very sweet."

Sophie looked my way, her face all aglow from that happy thought. I wrinkled my nose at her.

Isabelle now turned to me, "Dawson."

I still didn't understand how she knew our names.

She continued, "I would like you to tell me about the first time you had a crush on a girl."

This caught me completely off guard. I found myself staring at her with a puzzled look on my face. I then said, "Okay...I was about eleven or twelve years old at the time. My brother and I would go down the street to play at a friend's house. Each time we walked up that long driveway, Heidi and Molly would come down to greet us, barking all the way, letting everyone know someone had arrived. Our friend's name was Bruce. The three of us would throw the football around, play catch with a baseball, or just hang out.

"Bruce had three sisters. Oftentimes we would try to talk them into coming outside to play a game of kickball or wiffleball in the front yard. The eldest sister, Linda, was a year younger than me. I know every time I ventured up that driveway, I wondered if I would see her on that day. She had a spunky attitude, a squeaky voice, and liked to remind Bruce that she was the boss, being a year older than him.

"After a bit of coaxing the girls would agree to come outside and play. Most of the time, Linda would be wearing her Daisy Duke shorts with a tight little shirt. We'd get a game of wiffleball or kickball going on the front lawn. After a few minutes, it was plain to see from the look in her eye that she was having fun.

"Linda had a walk that was all her own, and it drove me crazy. When we played wiffleball I would have one eye on the game and one eye on her, all the while, not letting anyone else know how I felt. I still remember her standing at the plate waiting for the pitch. As she waved the bat in her hands, her cute little bum would wave too. Then one day my family moved to another city, many miles away, and I never saw her again."

I stopped at that point while thinking to myself...*And to this day, she still wanders through my walls like a ghost.*

For a few seconds Isabelle sat there staring at me with a blank expression. Then a huge grin came over her face as she said, "I'm sure she does."

My eyes widened and my mouth popped open. Did she just read my thoughts? Is that how she knows our names?

Isabelle spoke, "Not only are your stories genuine, but they have warmed my heart. It is a treasure to be young. I will tell you all you wish to know."

I glanced over at Sophie with a mocking smile and tossed her a wink. She looked at me with a sour face and stuck her tongue out at me.

CHAPTER 10

I REACHED OVER and took Sophie's hand in mine, then turned to Isabelle, asking, "First of all, where are we, and what year is it?"

"You are in the village of Powhatan, outside the city of Richmond, in the year 1886." I felt Sophie's grip on my hand intensify.

"Would that be Richmond, Virginia?" I asked.

"Yes."

"So, we have traveled back in time and from Massachusetts to Virginia."

"That is difficult to accept, I know. But it is true."

Sophie looked at me sadly as she spoke to Isabelle. "We kinda had a feeling that's what happened. We just didn't know how far back, or where."

I turned my gaze back to Isabelle, saying, "There's something else that's been gnawing at me. When we came to your door, you knew our names. Then, when I finished my story a stray thought came to my mind. You seemed to be looking through me and answered what I was thinking. Did you read my mind?"

Isabelle was glowing with pride as she replied, "I was giving you bits and pieces, hoping you would catch on, and you did. You see, I was born with a gift. If I look into your eyes, I can tell what you are thinking."

I sat there stunned, just staring at her thinking, *That's an awesome power.*

She quickly responded, "It has its benefits."

I shook my head trying to clear my thoughts and looked away from her. It must have been funny because both girls giggled with amusement.

Sophie then picked up the interrogation. "We came here, believe it or not, in an elevator. It wrote a message to us saying that our only way back was to retrieve its key from someone. What is this all about?"

"Slowly, my dear," Isabelle said in a calming voice. "What did the message say, word for word?"

The elephant mind sprung into gear. "*He has my key...bestowed by the Watcher...take it away from him...it's your only hope for return... the bag outside will profit you.*"

Isabelle's eyes opened wide for a few seconds before settling back down. With a knowing smile she said, "He is wise, and he has chosen the two of you."

"I'm confused," Sophie replied.

"Allow me to explain. The one who has the key would be Voltaire. He's not going to give you the key, for he has other plans for you." Isabelle continued, "The Watcher is suitably named. He is an entity that observes the evolution of all things through time. He sees into the past, present, and future. The Watcher has a fascination with living things, in particular, mankind. He is neither good nor bad and merely observes.

"Although, there are times when he will indirectly tweak things just a bit. You see, sometimes mankind turns down a path toward total destruction. The Watcher can see how everything plays out from the past, through the present, and into the future. Not wanting his little gem to come to its end, he steps in and tinkers with the game board to influence an outcome. He never seems to directly participate. Instead, he uses others and chooses to remain on the outside, watching things play out.

"The Elevator serves as a herald to the Watcher. He's not alone. There are others like him. Yes, they can time travel, but they are more than just time machines. They are alive, incredibly intelligent, and resourceful. They are also able to take any shape or form they wish."

Isabelle rose from her chair, saying, "Let me pour us some tea. After that, I'll tell you the story of what I know. But first, I'm getting some confusing signals. Is your name Sophia or Sophie?"

"It's Sophia. He likes to call me Sophie. It's his way of putting an endearing twist on it."

"Ahh, now I understand," Isabelle answered. She then crossed the room and rescued three tea cups from the boredom of the cupboard. After placing them on the table she removed the soup bowls and brought the teapot over from the fireplace.

In Isabelle, I saw a luring feminine grace. Yes, she had a soothing, articulate voice and an attractive charm to her walk. But more so than that, with her subtle facial expressions and that soft glow in her eyes, she had a way of drawing you in and disarming you.

CHAPTER 11

AFTER POURING EACH of us some tea, Isabelle settled back into her chair. With both hands she gently raised her teacup to her lips, slowly taking that first hot sip before saying, "Now, I'll tell you my story.

"Twice, I remember, the Watcher employed the services of Voltaire and his crew. The first time was in the spring of 1776. There was to be a secret meeting of some of the colonial leaders. It would take place in a small town outside of Philadelphia. Men named Jefferson, Adams, and Franklin, among others, would be in attendance. Meanwhile, British spies had caught wind of it. A military unit consisting of Hessian and British soldiers was dispatched to make certain that everyone in attendance was either executed or imprisoned.

"Well, that military unit never made it to the meeting. They ran into Voltaire and his crew and were never heard of again. I know this to be true, because I was there that fateful day and witnessed the brutal carnage, firsthand. That day has been a scar on my memory ever since."

I sat further back in my chair and turned my head toward Sophie. Her face echoed my thoughts. *What the hell are we listening to? That was well over a hundred years ago.*

Calmly, Isabelle said, "Be patient my children, and allow me to explain. I was a young girl of sixteen at the time. My mother had made a fresh batch of candles, and I just finished delivering some of them to our neighbors down the road. I remember that daylight was getting thin. The sun had just gone down and dusk was now settling in. I was hurrying along the country road to get home before dark.

"I heard the sound of many boots running along the road behind me. I became afraid and darted off to the side of the road, hiding behind one of the trees. My heart was pounding. I tried to stay still, hoping I wouldn't be noticed. A moment later, I saw a group of British soldiers come running by. Each one of them had a rifle in his hands. Their numbers looked to be about twenty to thirty strong. I don't remember hearing any voices, only the heavy sound of their boots against the road.

"That all changed in a moment. After most of them had passed by me, I heard the hollo of other men, who came out from the woods up ahead. The soldiers came to a stop. I heard shouting from the front of the group. Then the soldiers raised their rifles and began firing at these men. There were six of them all together, but these were not men. The shots fired by the soldiers hit their targets, ripping apart flesh and making large wounds. However, the vampires were steadfast and unwavering as they pressed on, attacking the soldiers up front.

"I heard blood curdling screams as Voltaire and the others bit and tore the soldiers, limb from limb. They wasted no time, seeming to run right through the unit of soldiers. The soldiers tried to fall back. Screams of terror echoed as they fired their guns and then tried to fend off the attackers with knives and bayonets. It was all to no avail. The wounds inflicted upon the vampires began to heal instantly. They never faltered as they continued to massacre all twenty to thirty soldiers. It was all over in a matter of minutes."

Isabelle stopped for a moment as she took a deep breath and sighed. She then said, "Near the rear of the group, there was a very young soldier who was one of the last to fall. As he lie mortally wounded on the road, he happened to catch sight of me in the woods." Isabelle's eyes quickly teared up and her bottom lip began trembling. She paused for just a moment to wipe her tears and regain her composure before continuing. "The two of us locked eyes for a brief period as his thoughts reached out and touched me. He knew he was dying. He thought I was an angel sent down from above to guide him up to heaven. I felt so sorry for him, knowing that I couldn't help him. I started crying. He knew then, that I was merely a by-stander caught in a cross-fire. His thoughts told me to hide quickly and stay hidden. I slipped back behind the cover of a tree, but couldn't help myself from peeking around the side with one eye.

"I stood still, frozen, horrified, and white as a ghost, as the vampires were having their way with the bodies. Voltaire told the others to drag the remains into the woods. He then stopped for a moment, and I saw him sniff the air. Slowly, he turned to look straight at me. I froze in my tracks with fear, my pulse pounding, as he walked toward me. I was so terrified, thinking I was his next victim. He stopped right in front of me, eyeing me with a threatening gaze. With a cold and quiet tone, he said, 'You can come with me or suffer the same fate as them.' He raised his arm, pointing back toward the road littered with the soldier's remains. My only choice was to become his prisoner. Voltaire then escorted me back along the road to where his coach was hidden. Because of Voltaire's penchant for beautiful women, I remained alive. Although, I would never see my mother or family again. I cried for many months afterwards." Isabelle stopped for a moment to take another sip of tea. I glanced over at Sophie and noticed her wiping the tears from her eyes.

Isabelle continued, "Voltaire brought me back here to his mansion. Occasionally, he would drink of my blood, always from my neck. Unlike the others, he refuses to take blood unless it's from the neck.

"I would look into his eyes and read his thoughts, all the while, never letting him know that I could. The only one who ever knew of my gift was my mother. She told me that I possessed wondrous powers of vision and memory. She also told me to keep them secret and never let anyone know about them. She said, 'There are those who would accuse you of witchery, while others would imprison you to use your powers for their gain.' So, as time went on, I would peer into Voltaire's eyes reading his thoughts and moods.

"He loved me, and I grew fond of him. He was constantly urging me to become his bride. However, that would involve his turning me into a vampire also. I saw how the vampires lived and found it revolting. Therefore, I continued to fend off his requests. He could have forced me, but I knew from his eyes he wouldn't. He wanted me to willingly become his bride.

"Voltaire gave me small amounts of his blood, providing me with incredible regenerative powers, along with the ability to stay young and beautiful. I satisfied his needs while staying one step ahead of his moods. Deep inside, I resented that he had taken my life away from me. I also found it unpleasant to witness how cold and cruel he was to other humans."

Isabelle brought her story to a stop here, perhaps wrestling with her thoughts. She turned around to tend to the dwindling fire in the fireplace. While doing so, she asked me if I could bring a few logs in from the pile stacked just outside the front door. A teary-eyed Sophie rose from her chair and followed me outside. One by one, she loaded as many logs into my arms as I could carry.

50

CHAPTER 12

AFTER TOSSING ANOTHER log on the fire, I stacked half a dozen others off to the side of the hearth. We then settled back into our chairs, for Isabelle was just about ready to continue her story.

"The second time the Watcher used the services of Voltaire involved time traveling into the future. In order to accomplish this task the Elevator would be needed. Voltaire thought that his services deserved some sort of compensation. He brought this to the attention of the Watcher. The Watcher, in turn, offered him the Elevator as a gift. However, the gift carried with it one stipulation. Henceforth, once this task was finished, neither he nor any other vampire could enter the Elevator. Voltaire balked at this condition, saying, 'What good could it possibly serve me then?'

"The Watcher told him he could use the Elevator as a supply line. He could send it into the future to capture humans and bring them back to him. Voltaire would no longer need to hunt the streets of Richmond at night acquiring new victims to satisfy his blood supply. The Watcher added that this stipulation was not negotiable. This would be the only way he would offer this gift. Voltaire agreed, and the Watcher gave him a control key. It's a ring that he keeps in an amulet. Voltaire wears it on a chain around his neck.

"For the new task at hand, Voltaire was to bring the same five vampires that had participated in the raid on the British and Hessian soldiers. Voltaire also asked me to accompany him on the voyage. We were to travel to a small town in Germany. The year was 1943. There was a military facility in this town, where some physicists were working on a government project. They were only days away from the answers on how to create a nuclear explosive device. The physicists had no idea that it would be used with impunity, hundreds of times across the nations of the world. The group of vampires were to storm the facility, leave no survivors, and burn the building to the ground.

"I remember entering the Elevator with the others. It seemed like such a strange and futuristic looking vessel. I found it hard to believe that this odd contraption would be able to move or go any-where. However, it did, and as we moved I suddenly felt a presence coming from the mirrored wall. Gazing at myself in the mirror, I sensed that someone or something was looking back at me, through me, scrutinizing everything about me.

"When the Elevator came to a stop a voice from behind its walls began to speak. Everyone was startled by this voice without a visible body. It spoke to Voltaire, telling him that bringing me along was unwise. The voice reminded him that unlike the others, I was weak and vulnerable. It warned Voltaire that I would not survive this raid, dying in a clash with the soldiers. The voice then advised Voltaire to leave me behind, safe within the Elevator, until his return.

"Voltaire turned to look at me. Through his eyes, I read his thoughts. *'You mean so much to me. I brought you along for inspiration. I wanted you to see what I could do. But instead, I've endangered you.'* Voltaire let out a sigh of frustration. He then agreed to leave me behind.

"I was relieved. I did not want to see what was coming. They all lived and thrived on the carnage. I had seen more than I wished already. The Elevator door opened, and the others stepped out to embark on their raid. Seconds later the door closed, and the Elevator and I had a long conversation. A conversation that I remember as if it were yesterday."

CHAPTER 13

"ONCE THE DOOR closed and I was by myself, I asked the Elevator how it knew I would die in the upcoming raid on the project facility. The voice replied that it was merely a ploy to convince Voltaire to leave me behind. The voice said it wanted to talk to me alone. I asked the voice if it originated from a presence behind the mirror. As I peered at my reflection, I sensed something deeper on the other side.

"Strangely, the eyes of my reflection began to blink, yet mine were not. Then, a smile came over the face of my reflection, and it began to speak to me. I found it curiously odd and amusing, as I watched myself speaking back at me.

"With an awestruck gaze I listened, as the Elevator proceeded to burn each word it spoke into my memory. 'I sensed your ability to see into me when I scanned the seven life forms earlier. I blocked you from penetrating any deeper than you did. You possess a power that is very rare in humans. I scanned the thoughts and composition of all of you. I know your strengths and weaknesses, as well as your nature and feelings. The others are vile creatures. You, unhappily, remain a captive of Voltaire. Little does he know of the power within the gem he possesses. You have been wise to use this gift to navigate around him, unbeknownst to him. If he knew, he would exploit your powers to his benefit. As for me, I am one of the heralds that serves the Watcher. I have the ability to change size and take on different forms. I can travel through space and time, as well as blend into structures and surfaces. The reason I'm using an Elevator form at this juncture is because humans will show no reserve and walk right into my vessel without hesitation. I, much like you, am also unhappy. The Watcher has lent my services to Voltaire. Voltaire wants to use me as a supply line to bring him captives from the future. I do not wish to serve him. There are other events unfolding, far away and of a much larger magnitude. It is there that I am needed. Instead, I find myself here with my feet stuck in the mud, as your kind would say, while I serve this obligation. To this, I don't understand his reasoning. But, the Watcher knows much more than his herald. When I protested his decision, he told me that emotions run strong in me and advised that I keep them in check. He also added that I am the wisest of his heralds, and that is the reason he chose me. The Watcher implied that the task would only be for a short period of time; that he knew what he was doing.'"

Isabelle stopped for a moment. She seemed lost in a thought while staring down at her teacup. She then caught herself daydreaming and looked up at us with a sad expression. "Sorry. I was just thinking about what a short period of time really meant."

She blinked her watery eyes a couple of times and then continued on with her story. "I was told by the Elevator that Voltaire's feelings for me were strong, and he would never bring harm to me. The same could not be said for Darious, one of the other vampires. He harbored a fervent disdain for my refusal to accept Voltaire's offers. I was told to do my best to stay clear of this one.

"The Elevator went on to tell me of herbs and potions that would nullify Voltaire's trances and deter the vampires. He disclosed the power of silver and sunlight, and how they could be used to defeat them in battle. He spoke of the ring and taught me how it works. He then went on to reveal the power of Voltaire's blood. Lastly, the Elevator told me to hang on to my human nature. He said he would find a way to right the situation for both of us. The Elevator then said that the others had returned, and he would have to remain silent now. Our conversation ended and my reflection, once again, became just a reflection.

"The Elevator door opened and the vampires re-entered. They were loud and boisterous, bragging of their feats. Drifting in with them came a burnt, smoky odor, along with the smell of blood. The door closed and we were ferried back to the mansion. I never saw the Elevator again. I do know that, on occasion, it would bring people to Voltaire; fresh blood for the vampire cause.

"Eventually, Voltaire grew tired of me and granted my release. This, with the condition that I remain nearby, so he could feel my presence. And so it is that I remain in the village to this day."

CHAPTER 14

ALL WAS QUIET for a moment or two while Isabelle's words slowly sank in. Sophie then rose from her chair and went around the table to Isabelle. She gently hugged her and with a troubled voice began to weep. "It's so sad. You lost your family and never got to live your life. He kept you for so long." This, in turn, brought Isabelle to tears, and they both cried through the hugs. I got up, walked around the table, and placed a comforting hand on each girl's shoulder while the emotions flowed. The next few minutes were spent quietly consoling Isabelle.

Later, after the tears had subsided, we returned to our chairs while Sophie poured us another round of tea. This gave Isabelle a little extra time to regain her composure before continuing.

"So, you're saying the small amounts of blood that you occasionally took from Voltaire kept you young and allowed you to span all those years?" I asked. "If my math is correct you should be about a hundred and twenty-five years old, yet to look at you, you appear to be still in your forties."

"'That is correct, Dawson. In that minute that the Elevator scanned all of us, it came to know everything about us. My mirrored reflection told me of the power of Voltaire's blood. It also explained the quantity that was needed to turn me into a vampire. I understood, that when the occasion arose, a lesser dosage would be completely safe. So, being forewarned, I knew Voltaire was not tricking me when he offered a small amount of his blood. I was not afraid or hesitant to sample the dose he offered.

"I found that it would transform my body back onto its prime youthful state. I also noticed it gave me incredible healing powers. This went on for years, until he finally set me free, about thirty years ago."

"We have also been in that Elevator and have no reason to doubt you. Your story is quite amazing," Sophie said.

"I couldn't agree more," I added. "But, how did the vampires have such success in battle without incurring any casualties? They were far outnumbered by armed soldiers who were trained in warfare."

Isabelle replied, "The soldiers had weapons which were made for fighting other men. They had no idea what they were up against. Their weapons would inflict wounds that quickly healed right back up again. They needed to either cut the head off a vampire or use silver. Silver will burn and disintegrate the body tissues of a vampire. If the soldier's ammunition had been made of silver, without a doubt, the outcome would have been different."

Sophie and I turned to each other. The look on her face reflected the same inspired confidence that I now felt. It was a good feeling, hearing those words from Isabelle.

Sophie asked, "Is Voltaire stronger than the others?"

"Very much so. Voltaire is the oldest and purest of blood. He is far stronger than any of the others. He also has a power that the others lack. If you look into his eyes for a moment or two, he can place a trance on you. In this entranced state, he will have complete control over you. I'm the only one, it seems, that this power of his has no effect upon."

"What of the others?" I queried.

"I spoke of Darious, who cares little for me. There is also Lorcan, who has a craving for the blood of youngsters. He has a twin brother, Draven. The other two are Keos, a bald, large, barrel-shaped vampire, and Fenris, the shaggy, wolf-like vampire. These are the full-bloods. Any others would be hybrids converted over by Voltaire. They're not as powerful as the full bloods, but their strength is far superior to that of any mortal man."

Isabelle rose from her chair and stepped over to the window, peering out for a moment. "It's getting late," she said. "The sun is beginning to disappear over the horizon. The two of you should stay here tonight. You'll be safe here."

CHAPTER 15

IT WAS CERTAINLY a kind gesture for Isabelle offer us accommodations for the night. Much like Isaac, I'm sure she was taking a huge risk in doing so. Obviously, Sophie and I had no plans on where to spend the night. I looked over at her. With wide eyes she was eagerly nodding yes to me. Isabelle laughed at Sophie's expression and said, "It's all settled then. You can stay in the room over here to the right. I know it smells of garlic, but that is a good thing. It will keep them from catching your scent." Isabelle lit a small oil lamp and handed it to me. I wandered off to check out the room while Sophie and Isabelle chatted for a while.

The room was small, but clean and uncluttered. The scent of garlic emanated from strings of garlic bulbs hanging along the exterior wall of the room. A twin sized bed butted up against the interior wall, warmed by the fireplace. Next to it sat a chair and writing table. I set the oil lamp down on the table. Just above it a small mirror hung on the wall. To the left and right of this mirror numerous rough drawings of horses and village scenery had been tacked to the wall. Drawing must have been one of Isabelle's pastimes, I assumed.

The room had one lone window, without any glass. The two solid shutters on the outside had been pulled closed. The shutter handles were U-shaped and made of iron. They protruded into the room far enough for a board to be dropped between them and the sides of the window casing. No one could come in, but someone on the inside could get out. Although it be small and simple, the room seemed cozy and safe enough for me. I'm sure the two of us would be content for the night.

Sitting down on the side of the bed, I began to gaze at the flame from the lamp. I took a deep breath and exhaled slowly while running my hands up over my face and through my hair, thinking about all that had happened this day. I then remembered I had left the backpack in the other room. I went back out to the main room to retrieve it. Meanwhile, Sophie had decided to call it a night and followed me back to the little room. We thanked Isabelle and bid her a good night as we closed the door.

I sat down once more on the side of the bed and started to examine some of the items from the bag. I pulled out a scarf and ran it over my hands. It was so smooth and pliable, yet metallic and strong. I could see the shape of my knuckles coming right through it. I tossed it aside on the bed. Sophie, in turn, picked it up and began to play with it.

Next, I reached for one of the ammo magazines. I slid a couple of bullets out of it. The silver bullets were hollow pointed. When I shook one of them, I could feel the inside sloshing around. They must have a liquid center, I imagined. Considering what Isabelle had said, this would be ideal. If a bullet was solid and pointed, it might pass right through and out the other side of the body. These bullets, however, would enter the body, break apart, and splatter liquid silver throughout the body tissues. Holding the bullet up to the light of the oil lamp, I said, "These are some really awesome toys."

Sophie replied, "How do they compare to these?" I turned my gaze to her. She was naked from the waist up. She held the scarf from her right shoulder, draping it down across her breasts to her left hip. I could see her nipples coming right through the scarf.

I looked at the backpack, saying, "These are toys from the future." Turning back to her and gazing with a lust, I said, "Those, however, are gifts from the Gods!" A smile of approval lit up her face as she released the scarf, letting it slip down across her breasts to the floor below. Sophie's eyes took on a soft seductive glow and that smile on her face turned to a more serious look, one of urgency.

I rose and stood before her, gazing deep into her eyes. Slowly, tauntingly, our lips drifted toward one another, barely touching at first, then giving way to a warm pressing passion. I scooped her up and tossed her onto the bed.

CHAPTER 16

LATER, WE AWOKE to the sound of someone pounding on the front door. Quietly, the two of us slipped out of bed and swiftly began throwing our clothes back on. We heard the creaking sound of the hinges as the front door opened. This was followed by Isabelle saying, "Darious, what are you doing here?"

A deep voice responded, "Looking for a young man and woman, who got away from the mansion today. I thought you might know where they are?"

We quickly finished dressing, then wrapped the scarfs around our necks and started pulling weapons from the bag.

Isabelle tried to stand her ground, saying, "I don't know what you're talking about, and you're not welcome here."

Darious grew agitated, saying, "Ya know, I never liked you. Tonight seems like a good night to remedy that situation. I'm going to take you out to the forest and tear you apart, limb from limb."

"You know what Voltaire will do to you if he finds out."

"Well, maybe he won't find out." This was followed by the sounds of scuffling as Isabelle tried to resist. But Darious, with his incredible strength, dragged her right out the door.

We each holstered a pistol to our waist. Sophie slung the quiver of arrows over her shoulder and strapped the bow to the side of her thigh. I slid the sword's harness over my shoulder, followed by the backpack. Then, Sophie and I slipped out the door. We followed in the direction of Isabelle's voice as she protested being dragged away.

The moon was full tonight, giving us a better field of view and the ability to move at a faster pace through the forest. We soon came to the edge of a field. Isabelle and Darious were in the middle of the field, about fifty to sixty yards away from us. Isabelle had fallen to her knees, pleading with Darious.

I whispered, "They're too far away. We'll have to get closer for me to take a shot."

"He's in my range," Sophie said, looking at me with a smug smile. The bow quickly sprang to life. She drew an arrow from the quiver and took aim. I heard Sophie breathe out slowly as Darious raised his left arm to strike. She let the bow string slip from her fingers. In the blink of an eye the arrow struck Darious, hitting him in the left side of his chest. Darious spun halfway around, then stumbled backwards a few steps before falling to the ground.

I looked at Sophie with surprise, saying, "That was an awesome shot. Remind me never to get on your bad side." A proud smile came over her face as she tossed a wink back at me. She quickly holstered the bow, and we ran toward the two of them lying on the ground. I drew my sword as we approached, not trusting Darious.

Sophie tended to Isabelle, who was lying on the ground crying, but appeared unhurt. As I approached Darious I noticed a burnt smell in the air. Drawing closer, I could detect some hissing and spattering sounds coming from his wound. Smoke was trailing out from where the arrow lie embedded in his chest. He was staring straight upward toward the sky and showed no signs of movement.

A few moments later Isabelle rose to her feet, sobbing, as Sophie hugged and consoled her. Physically, she remained unhurt. Emotionally, she had received a thrashing.

Meanwhile, Darious's skin had begun to darken and shrivel. His body was now decomposing at a rapid pace. I felt quite confident that Darious would no longer be troubling anyone. With one shot, Sophie had accomplished more than a whole unit of trained soldiers. We had the Elevator to thank for that.

CHAPTER 17

WHILE STANDING OVER Darious's body I turned to look in all directions to make sure no one else was lurking nearby. With no one in sight, it appeared as though we were out of any immediate danger. Slowly, we began to make our way toward the edge of the clearing. I led the way, scanning the tree line for any signs of danger. Sophie and Isabelle talked softly as they followed close behind. Off to our left, cast by the light of the moon, our shadows drifted alongside.

As I scanned the dark emptiness that followed the edge of the forest, random thoughts began to wander through my mind. Don't ask me why, but I began to wonder if the Sox had won the base-ball game. I also noticed that Isabelle was no longer crying, and the tone of her voice had returned to normal. I stopped and turned to Isabelle, saying, "You sound as though you're feeling better now. That was pretty scary. Are you sure you're okay?"

She smiled back, "Yes, thank you, I am. That was a close call. He has never come to my house before. He caught me off guard. I shouldn't have opened the door."

"Well, you won't have to worry about him anymore," I replied. I turned my gaze back to the tree line and continued on, leading the way.

Isabelle was still talking to me softly. "I'm glad to be finally rid of him. I was always a bit afraid that I might run into him alone. Oh... And Dawson. What is a World Series?"

"Isabelle, you've got to stop doing that!"

"Sorry." She then turned to Sophie, whispering, "What is a World Series?"

"It's a game where men use a wooden club, called a bat, to hit a ball and then run from one base to the next. They score a run each time they reach the fourth base, called home plate. The team that scores the most runs wins the game."

"Why would he be thinking of that, at a time like this?"

"Men," Sophie replied. She shrugged her shoulders as she turned her hands outward, saying, "Who knows?" The two of them began giggling with amusement.

After passing through the wooded area, we came upon the edge of the village. From there, we heard a commotion going on up ahead of us. A mother had a baby in one arm and was holding a young boy's hand with the other. A larger figure was clutching the other arm of the young boy. He seemed to be arguing with the mother.

From behind me, Isabelle whispered, "Lorcan."

Preoccupied with their argument, they hadn't noticed our approach. As we drew closer, I could see that the mother and the young boy were crying. I heard Lorcan say, "Be thankful I only take the boy, and not the baby too."

Lorcan's words infuriated me. Yeah, you might say they pushed me over the edge. I drew my pistol and fired twice, both shots hitting Lorcan in the chest. He released the boy and began clutching at his chest with both hands. Lorcan stumbled off to the side a few steps before tumbling to the ground. The young boy cried as he clung tightly to his mother's side, his face buried in her dress. Isabelle advised the mother to hurry home with her children and bar the door. Sophie stayed right behind me as I approached Lorcan's dying corpse.

From out of nowhere, something startled Sophie causing her to cry out. I turned to see another vampire. He had grabbed her by the arm. The two of us locked eyes for a moment, he then bared his fangs and hissed at me. Instinctively, I reached over my shoulder and drew my sword, bringing it down hard, slicing right through the vampire's arm cutting it off close to his shoulder. Sophie screamed and shook her arm free of the dismembered limb as it lost its grip and tumbled to the ground. The vampire let out a blood curdling scream and bounded off into the woods. I pulled Sophie close, then quickly turned my head looking for others. There was nothing to see except a smoldering Lorcan and a leftover arm.

Isabelle said, "We're not safe out here. It's best we hurry back to my house."

As we crossed the center of the village I began to reflect on what had just happened. It bothered me that this vampire had snuck right up next to us without our noticing. I had been totally focused on Lorcan's body and let my guard down. Lucky for us, he chose to grab Sophie by the arm and not bite first. I have to remember to stay sharp, watch the periphery, and not let that happen again.

Once we reached Isabelle's house, I opened the door to let the two girls enter first. The fire in the fireplace was still going strong and lit up the room. I followed them in and then set the board in place to bar the door. When I turned around, I saw an expression of terror on the girls faces as they looked back at me. That's the last thing I remember.

CHAPTER 18

I AWOKE TO the warmth of the fire, along with a throbbing pain coming from the back of my head. I was lying on the floor in front of the fireplace. There were pillows tucked under my back and head. I felt woozy and my vision seemed out of focus. Everything seemed distant and I felt disconnected, as if I were looking at everything through a window. Isabelle was kneeling by my side. I could see her lips moving, but couldn't make out what she was saying. There were tears in her eyes, as if she had been crying. She was gently stroking my head with a cool wet cloth. The damp coolness from that cloth felt soothing against my skin. The last I remember, I was over by the doorway. She must have dragged me over here.

Gradually, things started to get a bit clearer. My thought process began to shift gears and come out of slow motion. I regained some of my focus and could now hear Isabelle talking.

"Dawson, can you hear me?"

"Uh-huh."

"Try not to move just yet. Here, I want you to smell this." She was holding the root of some sort of plant in her hand. She snapped it in half before placing it under my nose. A strong peppermint smell shot through my sinuses. In that instant, the fogginess that had been hovering over me disappeared. My vision improved and my senses seemed sharp once again. However, the back of my head continued to pulse with a throbbing pain. Gingerly, I rose to a seated position. Reaching back with my left hand, I gently inspected the lump on the back of my head.

"That's a pretty big bump. Are you in a lot of pain?" Isabelle asked.

"Just, a nagging throb. I'll be okay."

"I have something that might help that," Isabelle said. She got up and went over to the counter. She returned with a small bottle of light green, oily liquid. Isabelle carefully poured some into her cupped hand. She then dabbed some on her finger and gently applied it to the bump and the surrounding area.

"Where's Sophie?" I asked.

"Voltaire has her. It was he that struck you on the back of your head."

My eyes narrowed as a scornful frown came over my face. "I've got to go after her. Is she okay? What happened after he hit me?"

She spoke as if it were a dream, not leaving out a detail. "Sophia cried out as she ran to your side. Voltaire took her by the arm and lifted her to her feet. She resisted, but he was far too strong. He held her by the arms in front of him. She was crying and looked at him with a loathing expression. Voltaire looked into her eyes and told her he was hosting a celebration tonight at his house. He asked her to come along as a guest. The expression on Sophia's face melted into a blank stare. Voltaire then released her arms, for she resisted no longer. Sophia stood relaxed, deep in a trance, under Voltaire's control. She stared straight ahead, her expression empty and indifferent.

"Voltaire then looked down at you, saying, 'See what you get for running away. Now that I have her, you'll come crawling back.' Voltaire next turned his gaze to me. With narrowed eyes he said nothing, but his thought was...*How could you?* He then told Sophia to come along. Obediently, she followed him out the door."

I stared into the fireplace. The throbbing from the back of my head was no longer of any concern. Sophie was now a captive, totally under his control. Then, a thought came to me. I took a deep breath, exhaled slowly, and gathered myself to my feet. Turning to Isabelle, I said, "You mentioned a potion that would negate the effects of Voltaire's trance."

"That's right...The Elevator told me how to prepare it. I have a bottle of it over here." I followed her over to a shelf with bottles of various colored powders and liquids, all sealed with corks. She picked up a small bottle of clear liquid. "This is the one. A couple of spoonfuls should protect you for about twenty-four hours."

"Are you sure it works?"

"No. I never really had any reason to use it."

I looked at her puzzled, then remembered she was immune to his trances. "You followed the Elevator's directions to a tee?"

Isabelle lowered her brow and pursed her lips together, scolding me with her facial expression.

"Okay," I laughed. I eased the cork out of the bottle and downed a couple of sips. The potion had a fiery bite, much like a strong whiskey. It left a hot cinnamon taste lingering in the back of my mouth.

"Whoa. That stuff's got some kick, with a nice after taste. Are you sure you're not running a moonshine still, out back in the woods." Isabelle began laughing at me. I pressed the cork back into the bottle and slid it into my pocket.

Picking up the backpack, I reached in and took out all of the ammo magazines and began stuffing them into my coat pockets.

"Aren't you the least bit afraid?" Isabelle asked.

I gave her a puzzled look. With a serious tone I replied, "Yeah. But, I can't let that get in my way."

"How do you handle it so well?"

"I do my best to push fear to the side, so I can stay sharp and focused. Fear can be a killer. And everyone fears something."

Isabelle continued to look at me with a troubled look on her face. I took the unzipped empty backpack and slid it down over the hilt of the sword on my back. The backpack's color blended right in with my coat. It was a bit crude, but it did conceal the weapon. When I turned, I noticed Isabelle slipping her coat on. "Where do you think you're going?" I asked.

"I'm coming with you."

"Ahhh," I growled, turning my head to the side. I then looked back at her with a disgruntled glare.

"I may be of some help. Besides, he won't hurt me."

I continued to stare with disapproval.

With a playful coyness, she said, "Well, I'm coming anyway, whether you like it or not!"

I couldn't hide my smile. Her mannerisms were pleasantly amusing. I knew there was no stopping her. In the back of my mind I also knew she might be a great deal of help. Isabelle was quite familiar with the mansion. She knew its layout, as well as its inner workings, and cast of characters. "Alright, you win," I said. I opened the door for her with a smirk on my face. "Let us be off...My Lady."

Being playful, she said, "Why thank you, dear sir." She then gestured with a little curtsy, and out the door we went.

CHAPTER 19

THE MOON AND stars seemed to be working far above and beyond the norm tonight, impressively lighting our way as we followed the road out of the village. I began to wonder if this was how it always was in this time period, unlike the age that I'm used to, with all those city lights reflecting off a more polluted atmosphere. Far off in the distance, I could hear the howling of wolves. That's not a sound I'm accustomed to hearing, and I must say, it rattled me a bit. However, Isabelle seemed quite relaxed and at ease with it. This served to remind me that we're each a product of the world we grew up in.

Quietly, I looked to the stars, thinking of Sophie. I was worried about her. This turn of events was just what we didn't want to happen. We were supposed to stick together at all times. I didn't like the fact that she was now a captive, separated from me in the face of all this danger. Whatever it takes, I have to find a way to rescue her. I only pray there's still time.

"Dawson," Isabelle said.

"Yeah."

"I have to tell you that while you were lying incoherent in front of the fireplace, I looked into your eyes and saw your stray thoughts flashing by."

I turned my head and gave her a stern look. With a sheepish manner Isabelle turned her gaze away.

"And," I said.

"Well, I saw you running toward a metal coach that had no horse. You entered the coach and it began to move rapidly on its own. Strangely, you were talking to it, and it was talking back to you. There was a wheel in front of you and as you turned it the entire coach responded by turning also. I saw many houses that seemed so close together and others that were incredibly tall. Then, the thought slipped away.

"Next, you were sitting in a room watching a box that had little people in it. They were talking and moving around, but couldn't come out of the box. Is this what the future is like? Do you shrink people down and keep them in a box? It seems like a cruel form of entertainment."

I laughed as I turned to her. "In the future our carriages operate without horses. We have radios and phones, like this one." I pulled my phone from my pocket. "I can push a couple of buttons and instantly talk to someone on the other side of town or, for that matter, to someone on the other side of the country." Isabelle's eyebrows raised and her mouth popped open with an expression of amazement. "The people in the box are not really in there," I said. "The box spins pictures so fast that they seem to blend together creating natural movement. Voices and sounds are added to tell a story.

It's much like your dreams or someone's thoughts are being played out inside of the box."

"Why are your roads black?"

"Asphalt. It's like liquid rock that they pour over a road. The workers shape it and flatten it out. It quickly hardens and becomes solid as a rock. It allows us to travel smoother and faster without losing control. There's no more fighting the mud and dust, along with those wagon ruts. And the houses seem close together because in the future we're crowded with a lot more people."

"There was one other thought that surfaced. You were lying on a bed with Sophia and being playful. You told her you were going to give names to her legs. The left one was Christmas and the right one, New Year's."

"Whoa...Whoa...Whoa," I interrupted. I was laughing as I turned to face her, saying, "No need to go any further. I don't think I want to know how much you saw."

Isabelle bashfully looked down and whispered, "I'm sorry." She then turned her head, ever so slightly, gazing up at me with a playful innocence in her eyes.

I was smiling on the outside while fighting back the laughter on the inside. I looked at her thinking, *Dangerous, yet sooo... charming.*

"Thank you," she whispered.

She caught me off guard again. "You gotta cut that out," I said, shaking my finger at her while trying to hide my laughter with a mock angry face. She knew I was playing and laughed back at me. As we continued walking, I made sure I was facing forward while I thought, *It would not be an easy task, to be the man in her life. I* then asked, "Do you ever find yourself wishing there was a man you couldn't read?"

"'There are times when the thoughts I see are cruel and frightening. Why do you ask?"

"Well, if there was someone you couldn't read, you wouldn't always have the answers up front. For instance, let's say someone gave you two presents. The first one is unwrapped. Instantly, you know what it is. The second present is in a box wrapped up with paper and a bow. It leaves you with a sense of wonder as you pull away the layers to find out what's inside."

"I often wonder what my life would have been like if I hadn't run into Voltaire."

"I'm sorry. It was not my intention to make you sad."

"I find it sweet of you, that you consider my feelings. I'm not sad at the moment. I just wanted to show you, that even though I find answers fast, I still wonder as much as you."

I smiled and nodded at her. I then looked to the stars once more, wondering about Sophie and what lies ahead.

CHAPTER 20

As we came around a bend in the road, Graveswood mansion came into our view. Earlier in the day this mansion had appeared dull, worn, and gray looking. But now, in the moonlight, it was all aglow and bustling with activity. Every light inside the place must have been on. Once we reached the iron gates, we turned in and started up the driveway toward the house.

I asked Isabelle, "How long has it been since you were last here?"

"I've passed by, and I've seen Isaac. But, I haven't been inside for close to thirty years."

As we passed between the willow trees and drew closer to the front porch, I could hear the sound of music playing inside. Isabelle and I started up the front stairway. Strange it was, I thought, that to this point we still hadn't encountered anyone. I'm sure that Voltaire anticipated my arrival. However, there were no sentries keeping watch by the front gate or the front door. Everyone was inside. Then, I remembered Isaac's words, "Lion's den." They were fearless and welcomed any fool that showed up at their front door.

This was not a comforting thought, as we were standing right in front of it. Mounted on the door was a heavy iron knocker with the intimidating face of a gargoyle. I reached up and lifted the heavy iron knocker with my hand. As I did so, Isabelle quickly blurted out, "Are you sure you want to do that? I mean... Walk right in through the front door."

"I don't think we're surprising anyone. Why? What do you have in mind?"

"Well, it's obvious that the celebration is going on in the large room to our left. But, the room over here to our right is silent, and the windows are dark. We could slip in unnoticed."

I then had second thoughts and eased the knocker back down. "Alright. You know the room layout. We'll try it your way."

*   *   *

We moved along the porch over to the first window on our right. I quietly slid the window upward and crawled in. The room was huge, dark, and as far as I could see, empty. I reached back and took Isabelle's hand, helping her as she crawled through behind me.

Over to our left, I could see light from out in the hallway sifting through the cracks that outlined a set of double doors. Quietly, I eased one of the doors open just a bit, to peek out into the hall. Isaac was standing there giving instructions to another man who appeared to be one of the servants. After this servant turned and headed out of the room, I opened the door further and whispered, "Isaac."

Isaac turned, but when he recognized me a sad look came over his face. His eyes then opened wide as he noticed Isabelle peeking over my shoulder. Immediately, a smile came to his face, and he rushed over to us.

"Isabelle, it's so good to see you again. Come in...Come in."

As we were stepping through the doorway, Isaac quietly said to me, "He's expecting your arrival."

I replied, "Well, I'm not one to disappoint him." I then reached up and felt the lump on the back of my head, saying, "After all, he did go out of his way to hand deliver my invitation." I then smiled and continued past him, saying, "Besides, I love a party."

Isaac closed the double doors behind us. We were now standing in a large front hall that reached all the way up to the second floor ceiling. About twenty feet in front of us a beautiful, wide, white stairway led up to the second floor. Elegant banisters decorated both sides of this stairway, flowing down to its wide base where they curled outward on each side. At the top of the stairway the banisters continued off to the left and right, forming a balcony on either side overlooking the hall and front door below. To the left and right of this wide stairway, narrow corridors led back toward the rear of the house. Large tapestries decorated the walls of this huge open room. Also hanging on each wall, near the base of the stairway, was a shield with two swords crisscrossed behind it.

Over to our right were the doors we just came through. To our left, the double doors were open to a room filled with music and the loud banter of voices. A celebration of some sort was taking place.

Isaac said, "Follow me. I'll show you to your table."

"It appears we have reservations," I jokingly whispered to Isabelle.

"I guess that means we could have come right through the front door after all," she answered.

"I really wanted to give that knocker a try," I mumbled.

As we entered the room those loud voices we heard from the hallway grew silent. All eyes seemed to take notice of us. The only sounds I now heard came from the musician. Yeah, this was certainly an awkward moment. The staring went on for the next few seconds as we began to cross the room. Then, all at once, the loud chatter and laughter returned. Everyone had resumed their conversations, no longer paying any attention to us. I would have preferred a more inconspicuous entry, slipping through the crowd unnoticed to our table. However, that seems to be the way our luck was running.

The room was large and quite elegant. Tall windows were richly adorned with long red draperies. Polished brass gas lamps hung from the walls, flooding the room with light. The wood floor must have been freshly waxed or oiled, for it shined brightly under the light from these lamps. I counted eight large round tables spread out across the room. On each table there was a basket of bread, a platter of cheese, and a couple of bottles of wine. Most of the tables were already filled with people, drinking and talking merrily as the music played. The source of this music was a lone musician nestled in the corner, bow in hand, massaging the strings of his violin.

Across the room, I saw Sophie seated at a table by herself. The mere sight of her ignited a warm feeling in me. She was looking at me, and for the next moment or two I was so focused on her that I no longer saw or heard anyone else in the room. I must have stopped in my tracks. I say this because Isaac tapped me on the arm and waved at me to continue following him as he ushered us toward her table. As we drew nearer, I could see there was something different about her. She was watching us approach, but had no expression on her face.

I sat down next to her with my back to the wall, giving me a full view of everyone else in the room. Sophie was seated to my left. Isabelle took the chair to my right.

I turned to Sophie and asked, "Are you alright, sweetie?" She didn't respond. She just looked at me as if I were a stranger. "Sophie, it's me, Dawson. Are you okay?" The response was still the same.

Isabelle leaned over to me, saying, "It's no use. She can hear you, but she's unable to respond as you wish. It's the trance that she's under. She has no choice but to follow Voltaire's commands and do as he wishes."

CHAPTER 21

A HOLLOW FEELING crept over me as I sat looking into Sophie's blank face, seeing nothing but an empty stare. I'm used to seeing her eyes light up, or be angry, or look at me as if I'm completely crazy. This expression was distant and cold, and I could feel the pain deep in my heart.

Sophie still had the quiver of arrows on her back. Her hair and coat collar hid the better part of her neck, but down below her chin, I was able to see the scarf still wrapped in place. I reached under the table and peeled back her coat. The gun remained on her hip, and the bow was strapped to her thigh.

Isabelle leaned toward me again, saying, "They have nothing to fear from her weapons. She's totally under the control of Voltaire."

"Does the trance wear off?"

"In a day or two."

"Let's see if we can speed that up a bit." I reached into my pocket and retrieved the small bottle of potion. While keeping it concealed in my hand I reached for a bottle of wine and uncorked both of them at the same time. While trying not to draw any attention, I slipped half the bottle of potion along with some of the wine into Sophie's glass. Next, I poured Isabelle and myself each a glass of wine. Isabelle and I raised our glasses encouraging Sophie to drink a toast with us. She did so, sipping a little at a time until her glass was nearly empty.

I turned my gaze to the rest of the room, asking Isabelle, "Which one is Voltaire?"

She discreetly pointed to a table up front. "The one seated between the two women is Voltaire."

Voltaire looked more like a pirate to me than a vampire. He had shoulder length dark brown hair, with a short dense beard. His skin was tanned, not pale as I had expected. He wore a billowy white shirt, and a small loop of gold decorated his left ear. Voltaire looked remarkably young, perhaps late twenties to early thirties. This took me by surprise. I had assumed that he would look much older, considering all those years he has under his belt.

"Who are the others?" I asked.

"The women on either side of Voltaire would be his wives. The vampire with the missing arm, who is staring at us now, is Draven. Keos is the large bald one. Fenris has the beard and shaggy hair."

"So, all the full-bloods are at that table?"

"That's correct."

"What about these other people? Are they the blood supply; the unfortunate victims that the vampires choose from?"

Isabelle turned her head to face me. "Everyone seated in this room besides you, me, and Sophia, would be vampire."

My eyes opened wide as I scanned the room, saying, "That's encouraging."

"Yeah. The deck is heavily stacked against you. It's a good thing I came along."

"Oh...I feel better already," I teased. "There's close to forty of them and only two of us. Maybe three. We've got a lot of silver, but only two guns. We won't be able get shots off fast enough. There are a number of gas lamps here. Does fire pose a problem for them?"

"No. Not at all."

"Why am I not surprised?" I muttered.

"The two wives and everyone else in the room would be hybrids, converted over by Voltaire. They're not as strong, but still vampire and deeply devoted to serving him."

"Great...Here I was thinking they might be of some help to us, only to find out they're all tucked in his corner."

"How's your confidence level now, Dawson?"

"Stirred, not shaken," I replied with a smile, as I sat musing about what the reverse of that brought to my mind.

Isabelle smiled at me and teased, "You don't have a plan. Do you?"

I took another sip of wine and said, "The plan is to look for openings and make adjustments on the fly."

"I knew you didn't have a plan," Isabelle said, biting her lip to hold back the laughter.

CHAPTER 22

I TURNED TO Sophie while questioning Isabelle. "She still looks like she's under a trance. I gave her quite a bit of that potion. Are you sure it works?"

"It keeps you from falling under a trance. I'm not sure if it brings you out of one."

"That's reassuring, seeing as how we're so outnumbered. So... You say she can hear me. But, does she fully understand what I say to her?"

"Yes. She will understand exactly what you say, but her mind can't find the connection to respond as she or you would like."

I leaned over and whispered in Sophie's ear. "I love you, sweetheart. We're gonna find a way out of this. Voltaire has you under a spell or trance. If you find yourself coming out of it, signal me, but don't let Voltaire know he's lost control." I reached under her coat and removed the pistol from her holster, then brought it under the table to my lap.

"Isabelle, have you ever shot a pistol before?"

"No." She was wide-eyed and apprehensive.

"This type doesn't have a safety. You just point and shoot. The first shot will take a hard pull on the trigger. Each shot after that will come easy, only needing half as much strength as the first trigger pull. Aim for the center or trunk of the body. All these bullets are made of liquid silver. One shot should be enough to drop anyone. You have fifteen rounds in the gun.

"We're heavily outnumbered, and with Sophie still entranced, I need to increase our odds. If things go wrong, remember, it's either us or them. You can do this...Right?"

"I think so."

I slid the gun over to her lap. "Good. Get a feel for it in your hand, then slip it into your pocket. You're going to have to move fast if I decide to stir things up. Stay close to me. That way we have each other's back, and I can reload for you."

Servants came out of the kitchen with trays of food, stopping at each table to deliver their bounty. The servers were friendly and courteous as they arranged the large platters of food upon the table. There was a choice of lamb or beef, with potatoes, gravy, and biscuits. One thing was for sure, with plenty of food available, Voltaire's kitchen did not skimp on the portions. I couldn't imagine that these servants worked here for money. Their role was probably more like one of a slave in the service of a tyrant. Like Sophie, maybe he had them caught up in a trance also.

I turned to Isabelle, saying, "What's wrong with this picture? We're sitting in a room full of vampires, who are eating normal food."

"They're just warming up. There is a room full of innocents, on which they will pray upon later."

"Do they do this often?"

"The parties are rare. They have something to celebrate tonight. I'm not sure what it is. As for feeding on the blood of others, that's usually done every week to ten days."

"So, could it be that we're not on the menu tonight?"

"It's a celebration. They'll all be drinking blood tonight."

Once Voltaire finished his meal he got up and began moving from one table to the next, greeting his guests with his wives by his side. His table was the first to be served and thus finished ahead of the rest of us. I kept one eye on Voltaire while finishing my meal. I watched as he slowly moved from one table to the next, mingling with his guests. He seemed to have a loud and boisterous manner about him. I also noticed an amulet hanging from a gold chain around his neck. This was the amulet that holds the ring, our only chance of getting back home.

CHAPTER 23

OUR TABLE WAS the last one visited by Voltaire and his wives. As he approached, I noticed a cocky, confident grin on Voltaire's face. His eyebrows were dark and heavy, his eyes a steel gray and powerful looking. I had to remember not to lock eyes with him, just in case this potion wasn't up to snuff. Upon reaching our table, Voltaire said, "I knew that by taking her, you would come peacefully. My name is Voltaire." He held his arms out wide and looked around as he proudly proclaimed, "Welcome to my home."

I replied with a brazen tone, "People call me Dawson." Then with a subtle shift of my head to the left, I said, "This is Sophia, and I believe you already know Isabelle."

Voltaire gazed uncomfortably at Isabelle for a moment, before quietly saying, "You could have been with me." He then turned back toward me and with a happier tone said, "Allow me to introduce my brides. This is Corin. She has been with me for twenty years now." Corin was tall and lovely, with long dark hair and brown eyes. "And this is Hanna. She is my new bride of one month. To this, we cele-brate tonight while the moon is full." Hanna was also beautiful, with long blond hair and deep blue eyes. Voltaire gave them each a small slap on the butt and told them to head back to the table. He watched them walk a short distance before he turned to sit down with us.

"So, Dawson, how was your walk here?"

"It took no time at all. I found myself pleasantly amused, caught up in conversation with my lovely friend." It was obvious that he still harbored feelings for Isabelle, and I couldn't resist turning the screw a bit.

Voltaire quickly shot Isabelle a scolding glare. He then turned back to me with a smile and said, "It's such a beautiful night out there, with the moon so full. Did you know, Dawson, this is my favorite time of year, autumn, with its cool temperatures, clean crisp air, and the changing of the leaves."

With a slight grin, I replied, "I find myself partial to Christmas and New Year's, especially the time spent between them." Isabelle immediately gave my leg a kick underneath the table. She was begin-ning to turn red as she tried her best to hold back her laughter.

"Am I missing something?" Voltaire asked.

"No. But he is," I replied, as I saw Draven strolling toward our table. He was staring at me with scornful eyes.

Voltaire introduced us. "Dawson, I'd like you to meet my friend, Draven. He had an unfortunate accident earlier this evening."

I stood up and said, "Sorry to hear that, my friend. No hard feelings I hope," as I reached out to shake what wasn't there. Draven grew enraged, baring his teeth as he swiftly leaned across the table bringing his face up to mine and letting off a low husky growl.

"Draven!" Voltaire intervened. "Enough. Now is not the time or place. Return to the table and cool off." Draven retreated back to his table, grumbling and shooting me scathing looks along the way.

Turning to Voltaire, I said, "Your friend seems a bit temperamental. I don't think he likes me."

"I can't say that I blame him. It's lucky for you that he respects me. It would do you well to do the same. Earlier tonight, he let his guard down in a fair exchange between the two of you. He lost a limb in the process. However, I must warn you, Dawson." Voltaire then leaned in closer and boldly glared at me as he said, "Draven is a formidable warrior that you should do your best to avoid encountering."

"I'll keep that in mind," I said, sitting further back in my chair, glancing from one side to the other, making sure I didn't lock eyes with Voltaire. Draven did not strike fear in me, especially now with no right arm. Voltaire, however, was a different story. He had intimidator written all over him. He was larger, stronger, bold and confident. He also had a menacing look to his face, along with those luring evil eyes.

I felt that Voltaire was becoming agitated with me. This was probably because I kept throwing off eye contact with him. He then chose another approach.

Voltaire turned to Sophie, saying, "Ahh Sophia, so young and beautiful. Do you know, Dawson, what I find to be the most enticing feature of a woman?" He stood up and walked around behind Sophie. "A young woman's neck is so soft, so warm, so vulnerable, and it carries her scent so well." He was glaring at me as he leaned over, slipping his hand under Sophie's hair. Voltaire was daring me to look at him, trying to ensnare me with this insidious, intimate behavior.

I knew full well he was baiting me. Yet, I still felt that jealous rage building inside of me. I have to give Voltaire credit. He knew how to push my buttons. I glared right back at him while muttering, "Now you're really starting to piss me off."

Voltaire continued to look at me and taunt me. He brushed back Sophie's hair and peeled open her coat collar. He drew his lips in close to her neck and whispered to me, "So tempting."

That was the tipping point. I reached for my gun. But before I could remove it from the holster, his lips brushed against the silver scarf. There was a hissing and spattering noise. Voltaire stood up quickly. He was stunned. His lips were bloody and ragged looking. He instinctively brought the back of his hand up to his mouth.

Voltaire quickly regained his composure, glaring at me fiercely. I could sense the heat of his rage building. I gave him no quarter, firing back a contemptuous stare. As he drew his hand away from his mouth, I was amazed to see that his lips were almost completely healed.

Voltaire summoned Keos from the table up front. Slowly, he turned back to us and said, "I am less than amused by your insolent behavior. I shall deal with you later." Voltaire addressed Keos as he motioned to Isabelle and me. "Take these two down below and put them with the others. And then, see if you can find out where the hell Darious is."

I slowly turned my head to Isabelle, with eyebrows raised, thinking; *they don't know about Darious yet. That's a positive. Less anger toward us, and more concern about trouble in their own ranks.* Isabelle, with a subtle purse of her lips, acknowledged the thought. I took my hand off my gun and placed it back upon the table. I considered it better to divide and conquer, than to try to take on this whole room, here and now.

Big, husky, barrel-shaped Keos pointed to me and then Isabelle, saying, "Follow me."

"What about Sophie?" I asked.

Voltaire replied, "She will remain here. I don't have to be concerned that she will interfere with our celebration."

As I stood up, I looked at Sophie with a troubled, uneasy feeling. How was I going to keep her safe if we keep getting separated? She was staring back at me, but not blankly this time. I thought I could detect the slight whisper of an expression, a yearning from her eyes.

Isabelle and I fell into line behind Keos, following him out of the room. While crossing the room, my mind began to wonder. Did that really happen, the look in Sophie's eyes, or was I just imagining it?

CHAPTER 24

ONCE OUT OF the room, my thoughts took a different path. I caught Isabelle's eye and thought, *No guns...Too much noise...I'll use the sword.* Isabelle grinned and threw a wink back at me. A smile came over my face while I slowly shook my head from side to side marveling at her talent.

Clueless Keos led us through the front hall and down the corridor to the right of the stairway. Keos stopped near a door to light a gas lamp. Next, he opened the door and motioned for us to go ahead of him. We proceeded down a wide, wooden ramp that had railings on either side. This ramp was about eight feet wide and built solid to handle heavy loads. Halfway down the ramp we came to a landing, where we turned to the left and followed the second half of the ramp down to the cellar. I couldn't help thinking that these wide ramps were designed to allow barrels or carts of goods to be rolled below for storage until needed by the kitchen.

As we came down to the bottom of the ramp I could see a light coming from the other side of the cellar. Quickly, it all came into view. A large portion of the cellar had been made into a cage that held roughly twenty to thirty people. Some of them stood around, while others sat on chairs or sofas. All of them seemed to have that same lost look on their face as I had seen earlier from Sophie.

A chain and padlock tightly secured the door of this cage. Keos instructed the two of us to wait right there by its door. Meanwhile, he lumbered over to a nearby table, where he placed the oil lamp down and picked up a ring of keys. Keos was huge and solid as a rock, but also a bit careless. While he fumbled with the ring of keys, looking for the right one, I noticed he seemed unconcerned with the two of us, or for that matter any of the captives in the cage. As Keos picked up the padlock with one hand and lined up the key with the other, I drew my sword and came down hard across both of his forearms, slicing one off and leaving the other dangling by loose flesh and tendon.

Keos reared backward, stunned, with a look of shock on his face as he viewed what was left of his arms. That's when I sprang forward and buried my sword into his huge barrel chest. Keos let out a grunt, then collapsed over backward slamming to the floor with a loud thump.

Oddly, the people in the cage were unmoved by the gruesome event they had just witnessed. They continued to sit around, aloof and vacant.

I turned back to Isabelle, saying, "So, this is where they keep the blood supply."

"Yes. They are fed and cared for by others during the day, so they may satisfy the vampire's needs by night. Voltaire keeps them in an entranced state. This keeps them from making any attempts to escape."

"In their condition they're more of a liability than a help to us." I picked up the ring of keys from the floor. "We'll have to come back for them later," I said, as I tucked the keys into my coat pocket.

"Well, at least that's one more of the full-bloods out of the way. But, where do we go from here?" Isabelle asked.

I grabbed the hilt of my sword and pulled it back out of Keos's chest. I then wiped the blade clean with his pant leg. "This guy's body is way too big to hide or drag far. It won't be long before he's missed. We need to get back upstairs now. I don't want to try to fight our way out of this cellar."

Isabelle retrieved the oil lamp from the table. Without wasting any time we quietly began sneaking our way back up the wooden ramps. I kept my sword in hand, ever ready, as we approached the door. In the event we encountered anyone, it would be more silent than a gun.

CHAPTER 25

ONCE WE REACHED the top of the ramp, Isabelle blew out the oil lamp and set it down. Slowly, I cracked the door open to make sure the path was clear. We then quickly followed the corridor back to the front of the wide stairway, only to find Draven standing there alone in the hallway.

A huge smile came over Draven's face. "Ahh...The moment is mine," he rejoiced. One-armed Draven stepped over to the wall and removed one of those swords that were crisscrossed behind a shield. He held up the sword while grinning at me, and said, "Now, we shall see what kind of swordsman you really are."

The loud chattering of voices and music echoing from the room next door drowned out the sounds of our confrontation in the front hall. My sword fighting skills were not well honed, but I wasn't going to back down from Draven. We began to circle each other. I lunged forward, thrusting my sword at Draven. He blocked my attack and countered with a swipe that sliced through my coat on the upper arm near my shoulder. Lucky for me, his sword hadn't penetrated deep enough to reach my skin. Again, I swung my sword on the attack. Draven easily blocked the path of my thrust. Then, with a little circling flick of his sword, he knocked my sword clean out of my hand and it clattered to the floor about ten feet away.

Draven sneered, "You are hardly a swordsman!" The expression on his face took a dark and wrathful turn. "Now, vengeance will be mine," he said. "I'm gonna slice your limbs off, one at a time, inflicting more pain into each wound as I go. I will see that you suffer an agonizing death. What do you have to say now, smart-ass?"

"You talk too much." I reached under my coat, drew my pistol, and shot him. Draven stumbled and fell back against the front door. I blew him a kiss good-bye with two fingers, then muttered, "Rot in hell, you maggot."

There was a brief moment of silence from the room next door. I looked toward Isabelle, saying, "Cat's out of the bag now." This was followed by the sounds of chairs tumbling and the scuffling of a herd moving our way.

I pointed to the top of the stairs and shouted, "Hurry. We'll have to take a stand from up there." Isabelle dashed up the stairway while I grabbed my sword and followed. I took the stairs three at a time, reaching the top just ahead of her. I knelt down to one side. Isabelle followed my lead and took the same position on the other side.

Looking down, I could see the room had spilled out into the huge hallway. Some of the vampires were already halfway up the wide staircase. The leader of the pack got to within about five stair steps from us when I fired my first shot. I hit him dead center at the base of his throat. A huge hole ripped open between his collar bones.

The force of the shot blew his body backwards and he tumbled back down the stairway knocking some of the others down along the way. Isabelle raised her pistol and began to fire. Vampire bodies dropped and tumbled back down the stairway, only to be replaced by others jumping over and around the bodies, trying to get up to us.

Off to my right, out of the corner of my eye, I saw something leap up and grab one of the vertical posts of the banister. It was Fenris, the wolf-like vampire. He had forgone the stairway, leaping right up to the second floor. Fenris slung his other hand over the top of the banister rail, in an attempt to pull himself the rest of the way up. I stood up quickly and swung my sword down on his wrist. The sword sliced right through his wrist, along with part of the rail. At the sight of losing his hand a look of shock came over his face. Fenris then toppled back down to the first floor.

"Dawson!" Isabelle yelled. "I'm out of bullets."

I reached into my pocket and pulled out two magazines of ammo. I reloaded my pistol and slid it across the floor to Isabelle, waving at her to slide the empty gun back. She quickly did so. But, before I could reload it I saw that Fenris was back again. He was standing on the other side of the banister. He held the hand rail with his one good arm while he took a wild swing at me with his mutilated arm. I leaned back as he did, and lucky for me he was missing that hand, for he just grazed me with that bloody stump of a wrist. I countered by lunging forward and slicing with my sword. I caught him just above the shoulder, taking his head right off. His headless body shook with a convulsive spasm for a few seconds, before collapsing and plunging down to the floor below.

Turning back, I noticed Isabelle holding her own against the onslaught charging up the staircase. The whole situation had them in a frenzy. They hadn't lost any of their determination to reach the top and disarm us. But, having to jump over and around the downed bodies along the way made this an increasingly difficult task. I popped a full magazine into my gun. Together, we took down what was left of the vampires below.

CHAPTER 26

A SMOKY HAZE hovered in the air around us, along with the smell of gunpowder and burnt flesh. My ears were still ringing from the gunshots. Smoldering bodies littered the stairway and floor below. The only sounds now came from the hissing and popping that emanated from their burning wounds. There must have been upwards of thirty vampires that lost their lives here. If it wasn't for the stairway, I doubt that we would have prevailed.

As I stood there surveying the carnage below, I asked Isabelle, "Did you see any sign of Voltaire?"

"No. Not Voltaire, or his wives."

"Well, it sure looks like the rest of the room poured out after us. I'll bet he's on the other side of that doorway, just waiting for us to come to him."

I reloaded both pistols with full magazines while we stood at the top of the stairs watching the bodies and the doorway below. I wanted to make sure the vampires had succumbed to their wounds before we began stepping over them. It was then that we noticed a hand holding a white napkin slowly extend through the doorway below and begin to wave.

"Step out and show yourself!" I yelled.

Slowly and tentatively moving around the door casing and into our view came a timid, frightened Isaac.

I whispered down to him while pointing toward the big room... "Voltaire?"

Isaac shook his head side to side, in the negative.

I asked again... "Sophie?"

His response was the same.

I finally asked, "Is there anyone else in the room?"

"All that's left, Mr. Dawson, is me and the fiddle player." The frightened face of the fiddle player eased around the door casing, along with a little wave of his hand. Isabelle started down the stairway.

"Isabelle...Wait. It could be a trap."

"No, Dawson. He's telling the truth." I followed her down, stepping over and around bodies until we were face to face with Isaac.

"Thank God, the two of you are okay. I can't believe my eyes. How could the two of you do all this?" Isaac asked.

"Tactical location and the right ammo," I replied. "Now, where's Voltaire and Sophie?"

"Voltaire took his wives and Sophia to the kitchen. They slipped up the back stairway. You know the way," he added, looking at Isabelle.

"Where does it lead to?" I asked.

"It bypasses the second floor and leads up to a room in the attic," Isabelle replied.

"Is there a way up to the attic from this stairway?" I asked, pointing back at the staircase behind us.

"No," Isabelle answered.

"Well then, we'll just have to follow their path. I guess it's up to you to lead the way...My Lady."

I followed Isabelle through the large function room, empty now, with overturned chairs and tables out of place. We proceeded down a corridor that brought us toward the kitchen. Warm air from the ovens in the kitchen radiated back through the corridor, along with the tantalizing smells of roasted lamb, beef, and baked bread.

The kitchen was enormous and surprisingly uncluttered. At its center was a huge counter top area for food preparation. A large metal rail hung down from the ceiling in a U-shaped pattern around both sides of the counter top. A variety of pots, pans, and trays were hanging down from this rail, providing ease of access while keeping the surface area of the counter uncluttered. Over to our left, there was a door that exited the rear of the house. Off to my right, there were two enormous cast iron cooking stoves.

Hearing a whimper, both Isabelle and I turned quickly to our right. How I didn't see them a moment ago, I'm not sure. But, there were three cooks cowering in a corner next to one of the stoves. Isabelle smiled at them, saying, "We're not here to harm you. Did Voltaire go out this door, or upstairs?"

One of the cooks slowly raised a finger pointing upward. "Thank you," Isabelle said. She then opened the door and stepped aside, saying, "You are free men now. Go ahead and find your way back home."

It was rather comical, the way the three of them moved away from the corner. They timidly inched their way out, slowly with cautious little steps, all the while, looking at us as if we were predators ready to pounce. Then, without taking their eyes off us, they grabbed what they could for pots and pans before dashing out the back door and across the field.

CHAPTER 27

ISABELLE PICKED UP a gas lamp and walked over to the wall, summoning me to follow with a wave of her hand. I looked at her as if she were crazy, thinking, *It's just a wall, and I do remember Isaac saying a stairway.* She smiled at me and then slid a wall panel open, revealing a hidden stairway built into the wall.

My eyes opened wide as I said, "Well, aren't you just full of surprises. I'm quite sure I never would have found this on my own." Slowly, I brought my index finger to my lips, saying, "As quiet as we can."

Isabelle nodded and we started up the narrow passageway, each quiet as dormouse, attentive to each footfall. The passage was extremely narrow, perhaps just over two feet wide. It made one turn to the right, about half the way up. I surmised that at that point we were between two different walls as we passed up through the second floor.

Reaching the top of the wooden stairway, we came to a small landing. About ten feet in front of us was a door. I caught Isabelle's eye and thought, *I'll go in first... You follow.* She lightly nodded, then we moved closer to the door.

The door didn't have a doorknob. It had the old-style thumb paddle latch. I drew my gun. Reaching out with my left hand I put my fingers around the handle and slowly pressed my thumb down on the paddle. I was hoping to quietly lift open the latch. Then it would only be a matter of swinging the door open, keeping the element of surprise in my corner.

As would be my luck, the door's thumb paddle wouldn't budge. I tried gently pushing in and pulling back on the door to see if I could free it up. My efforts were unrewarding. So, I applied a little more thumb pressure. Suddenly, the latch snapped open with a loud click. This wasn't what I was looking for. I had just lost the element of surprise. I threw the door open and burst into the room.

Voltaire had Sophie up against the wall, pinning her hands together above her head. I raised my gun toward Voltaire, only to see it slapped out of my hand by Corin. She came out of nowhere from behind me on my right. She must have been hiding all this time, off to the side of the doorway. Corin quickly latched a hold of my right arm.

Meanwhile, Isabelle had followed my coattails through the door. She was grabbed by Hanna from the left. Hanna slung Isabelle into the corner, where she struck the wall hard and crumpled to the floor. Hanna then grabbed a hold of my left arm. The situation now had obviously taken a turn for the worse.

CHAPTER 28

BOTH CORIN AND Hanna had incredible strength. The two of them barely exerted themselves, each holding an arm with one hand. I struggled, but within their grip it was as if I were bound in chains. It was frustrating to me, for I was much larger than them and yet they handled me as if I were a four year old.

Voltaire studied me with disdain. He told his wives, "Sit him in that chair, and don't let go of him."

There was a chair about eight to ten feet behind him, facing Sophie and the wall. Corin and Hanna dragged me over and plunked me into the chair. As they did, I noticed my gun lying on the floor next to it. The gun was so close, yet so far out of reach with the grip they had on me. Voltaire peered down at me. I angrily glared right back up at him. I could see a frustration boiling deep inside of him, probably due to his vain attempts at ensnaring me in a trance.

"You, Dawson, are a mere human, powerless in my realm. Yet, you insist on being a nagging thorn in my side. You have brought me much grief on this night of celebration. For that, I am going to let you watch as I take the pleasure of passionately drinking the blood from your loved one's soft, delicate neck. Then, she will obey my command and drink of my blood; enough to turn her into a vampire, right in front of you.

"Yes...I will have a trio of wives to serve my needs and satisfy my pleasures. Three wives will help me quickly breed new fullbloods, to restore the ranks of my brethren.

"As you watch, you'll see her fangs grow. Once turned, I will have her be the first to drink of your blood. But only a little, for then Sophia and I will watch as Hanna and Corin delight in drinking until there's nothing left in you."

Hanna and Corin, primed with anticipation, leaned in with their faces close to mine, baring their fangs and hissing.

"Once they've finished with you, I'll drag your lifeless carcass out to the forest, so the wolves can gnaw on your bones. It will be the perfect ending to your useless mortal life."

Voltaire turned away as he reached for a pair of gloves from a nearby table and slipped them over his hands. Sophie's back was against the wall, with her hands together high above her head. Voltaire moved back over in front of Sophie. He reached for the zipper of her coat and slowly slid it down, parting open the front. He peeled back the collar of her coat, exposing her neck wrapped in silver. Voltaire then delicately began unfurling the scarf from Sophie's neck.

As he did so, I peered into Sophie's eyes. She was looking directly at me in the same manner as downstairs; not as when we first entered the room, but as she did when I was getting up to leave with Keos. It wasn't that dull look at the field of view in front of her. Her eyes were fixed on mine, with a deep longing desire. I opened my eyes wide, raising my eyebrows, looking for any kind of a signal from her, but received nothing in return.

If only I had Isabelle's power of vision. I glanced over at her to my left. She had begun to stir, but still lay, out of sorts, crumpled in the corner. As I turned my gaze back to Sophie, I thought I saw her eyes blink at me. It happened only once, and so quickly that I couldn't trust my eyes.

Voltaire seemed to enjoy taunting me with his slow deliberate movements. He finished removing the scarf from Sophie's neck and turned to me. With a sarcastic smile he leaned forward, placing the scarf on my lap. "She won't have a need for this anymore. Now, I can see the beauty of her soft, young, tender skin. Her neck is so vulnerable, awaiting my plunder, forever more to belong to me." He was glaring at me, with those steel gray eyes piercing right through me. Still, the potion held true, keeping his trance at bay as I scowled back at him.

Isabelle had warned me that Voltaire was fiercely intimidating, and his strength outmatched the others by far. It was quite obvious that he knew it. It was as if he sought to use this lion-like intimidation to crush my brazenness, my nerve, and goad me into submission before he did away with me.

My insides were a churning mass of both anger and fear. But on the outside, I would only show him an expression of intense anger. This served to annoy Voltaire immensely. I knew the gratification he sought was to see me crumble with fear beneath him.

Voltaire, not seeming to get any satisfaction out of me, straightened back up and turned to Sophie again. He took her arms from above her head and moved them back down to the sides of her body. Voltaire now took the gloves off his hands and returned them to the nearby table.

While he did so, I looked into Sophie's eyes again and without speaking, I mouthed, "I love you." Her eyes became watery. Then, I saw a teardrop trickle down her cheek and fall to the floor.

I was getting desperate. My gun was out of reach, for I couldn't break the grips of Corin and Hanna. Isabelle had a gun, but was still too groggy. I needed to find a way to buy more time.

Voltaire reached up and turned Sophie's head to the side. Slowly, he began caressing the skin on her neck with his hand. I shouted, "Voltaire! Doesn't it make you wonder, how I was able to defeat the others so easily?"

"I would greatly appreciate it, if you would not interrupt me," he responded.

"I was sent here by the Watcher."

Voltaire, who had been leaning in toward Sophie, lifted his head up while still facing the wall. He exhaled with disgust. He then followed by saying, "What could you possibly know of the Watcher? He hasn't spoken with me."

"I know you served him twice; Once, against the English soldiers and then a second time against the German bomb program. I know that now he's unhappy with you and has sent me here to settle the matter."

Voltaire slowly turned around to face me with a wry expression on his face. He said, "Not good enough, Dawson. I don't believe you when you say you have spoken with the Watcher, for if you had, then you would know that four times I have done favors for the Watcher, not two." He glanced over at Isabelle. "She would only know of two times." Voltaire slowly turned his head back to me. He was gleaming with confidence. "I believe it was Isabelle you spoke with, not the Watcher."

CHAPTER 29

VOLTAIRE HAD SEEN through me and was calling my bluff. My mind was racing now, desperately trying to find the next move. I tried a different approach, saying, "I know about the amulet hanging from your neck and the ring that it holds. The ring that summons the Elevator, which won't allow you to enter, but brings humans to you. Isabelle doesn't know that, only the Watcher does." I smiled confidently now, knowing I had just hit a homerun

Sure enough, Voltaire fell for it; hook, line, and sinker. Voltaire's eyes narrowed and a grave expression came over his face. "If the Watcher wanted me gone, he would have sent a Titan, not a mere human. Look at you. You are powerless and pitifully remain subdued by my wives. I am in complete control of the situation. I have all the power."

I could sense the fury building inside of him like a tornado. His face was seething with anger. "If the Watcher truly did send you, then he gravely underestimated me. I will crush you here and now!"

Voltaire raised his right arm with his hand in a fist, over his head, ready to deliver a death blow.

But as he did, I heard the familiar sound of two clicks coming from behind him. It was sweet music to my ears. Voltaire heard it too. He froze for a moment looking puzzled. A split-second later, Sophie's arrow hit him square in the back. Voltaire's head and arms shot backward, as his chest heaved forward from the blow.

Voltaire let out a deep excruciating howl, startling Hanna and Corin enough to momentarily release me. I quickly drew my sword and plunged it deep into the side of Hanna's ribcage. Hanna was writhing with pain as she reached out with her hands, fumbling with the hilt of the sword. She stumbled off to the left and crashed to the floor.

I turned back to my right and reached for my gun on the floor. Corin was closer and had the angle on me. She quickly kicked my gun across to the far side of the room. Corin turned her head and glared at me. From out of nowhere she swung her arm up and back-handed me. The force of the blow sent me flying over the chair and across a table into a pile of baskets lying in the corner.

Sophie fired a second arrow, hitting Corin in the stomach just below the ribs. Corin let out a screech and immediately doubled over from the pain. She started to make gurgling noises and blood mixed with silver began flowing from her mouth. Unsteady and weak, Corin looked up at Voltaire for a moment, before collapsing to the floor.

Voltaire howled a second time as he saw his two wives go down, right in front of him. He was gritting his teeth and growling as he flailed his arms backward, trying to dislodge the arrow from his back. Sophie had hit him in the right spot, just out of his reach.

Smoke began to fume out of Voltaire's wound. I could hear it hissing like fat burning in a frying pan.

Voltaire turned awkwardly toward Sophie while spitting blood, and muttered, "You Bitch!"

Sophie shot him with another arrow, catching him in the chest, knocking him back three steps. She quickly drew and fired a third time, hitting him in the throat. Voltaire almost tumbled over backwards from the blow. As he turned to the side, I caught a clear view of how badly his throat was ravaged from that shot. There was a hole as large as a golf ball, with the skin torn and shredded around it. Thick black blood, dense and foamy, slowly oozed out from the wound.

I climbed out of the pile of baskets and bound over the table, glancing around the room for my gun. Voltaire reached up and ripped the arrows out from his neck and chest. He then slung them across the room. I saw him staggering and making gurgling noises as he tried to breathe. It appeared as though Sophie had inflicted enough damage. I felt certain that Voltaire would drop at any moment.

This was all short-lived though, for the gurgling noises quickly ceased. Voltaire's breathing was getting better, and I could see the wound on his neck healing quickly. My mind was spinning. I muttered to myself, "This is not good. She hit him hard, three times. That son of a bitch just keeps coming back. Wait till I see that goddamned Elevator. We could have used some bigger artillery. Maybe we do need a Titan."

Right before my eyes, Voltaire was recovering way too fast for comfort. In a matter of seconds his breathing was back to normal. His neck and chest wounds were almost completely healed. Only the arrow that was lodged in his back continued to do any damage.

Not seeing my gun, I grabbed Sophie's silver scarf from the floor. Voltaire was walking toward Sophie now. Sophie cowered back against the wall. He was almost upon her when I leaped from behind and wrapped the silver scarf tight across his face, pulling backward as hard as I could.

Voltaire bellowed out in pain as the scarf seared his face. He swung his arm backward, swatting me away. I tumbled across the room and crashed up against the wall. Meanwhile, Sophie crouched down and slid along the wall, out of Voltaire's reach.

Voltaire ripped the scarf from his face. Most of his skin came away with it. His face was just a mass of swollen, bloody tissue. Voltaire could no longer see. He was turning around, punching and grabbing with his arms, trying to catch one of us. I knew that I only had a few moments before his face would heal back up. So, I sprang to my feet and ran back toward him. I rescued my sword from Hanna's body and shouted his name, "Voltaire!"

He turned in the direction of my voice, swinging wildly with a punch. I leaned back far enough for him to miss. Before he could fire off another punch I swung hard with my sword, catching him just above the shoulder, slicing his head off. As if in slow motion, his body slowly tipped and then tumbled sideways to the floor. The battle had finally come to an end. I removed the amulet along with its gold chain from his body and stuffed them into my coat pocket.

The look of terror on Sophie's face faded to grief as she rose from her crouched position against the wall. She stared at me as I walked toward her. She was shivering, and her face was wrung out with emotion. I wrapped my arms around her. She hugged me like she never wanted to let go. Sophie gently laid her head on my shoulder, and the tears began to flow.

CHAPTER 30

I HELD SOPHIE close while she cried against my shoulder. "Ohh, Dawson. You don't know how horrible it was. I could see and hear you. But, as hard as I tried, my mind had lost control of my body. He told me to sit, eat, and drink, but speak to no one. I was so angry and frustrated. My mind was fighting to find the right connection that would allow me to regain control of my body." Sophie's crying grew heavy now. Her body shuddered as she gasped for breath in between sobs. I held her close and gently rocked her.

Meanwhile, Isabelle made her way out of the corner and over to Voltaire's body. She gently moved his head over to a more proper position, close to his shoulders. Isabelle removed the arrow from Voltaire's back, before carefully covering his body with a tablecloth. She knelt down beside his body. I saw her pull two small bottles from her pocket and reach under the tablecloth. I couldn't see what she was doing, but after a minute or two she returned both bottles to her pocket.

There was a sadness written across Isabelle's face as she took a moment to rest her cheek against Voltaire's shoulder. Isabelle then sat up, kissed her hand, and tenderly caressed his shoulder with it. She took a deep heavy-hearted breath and released it slowly while blinking her watery eyes. After sniffling a couple of times, she slowly rose and made her way over to Sophie and me. Isabelle wrapped her arms around the two of us and laid her head against our shoulders. A few moments later, she softly said, "This has been a very painful and trying ordeal for all of us. Why don't we go back to my house and get some rest. Tomorrow, we can come back and make things right here."

"You won't get any arguments from us," I replied. "I think all three of us are emotionally and physically wrung out. We've been through enough for one day."

I retrieved the amulet from my pocket and opened it up to verify that the ring was inside. Into my palm tumbled a ring made of a silvery-gray metal with a dark stone at its center. I gave a look toward Isabelle and she nodded her head in approval that this was indeed the ring. I tucked the ring back into the amulet before slipping it back into my pocket.

After wiping down my sword and Sophie's scarf, I searched the far side of the room for my gun. I found it nestled in a corner. "That reminds me," Isabelle said as she reached into her pocket. "Here, I think this belongs to you, Sophia," she added, handing the pistol back to Sophie.

"Thank you, Isabelle," Sophie said as she holstered the gun. The three of us then headed for the stairway.

"What about the people down in the cellar?" Isabelle questioned.

"I have the Elevator key and the key to the cage in the cellar. Once we've removed the bodies and cleaned up the hall, we can bring the captives up from the cellar. The Elevator can be used to ferry them back home to their proper places in time. They will be fine down there for the night. With any luck, by tomorrow, maybe some of those trances will have started to wear off."

Down below we found Isaac and some of the other servants beginning the process of dragging bodies out the front door to be loaded onto a cart. Isaac told us, "Go back to the village. Get some rest. We can't do much now with the darkness out there. We will load a few of these bodies, then wait until morning to begin again."

"That sounds good, Isaac. I'll be back in the morning to lend a hand," I said. The two girls and I started down the driveway toward the road.

Sophie was amazed by the carnage that was strewn across the front hall. She asked, "Just the two of you did all that?"

"Yup. Just the two of us," I replied.

"You must have had Angels on your shoulders," Sophie said.

"Or the guidance of a herald," Isabelle added.

"Do you really think he may have intervened?" Sophie asked.

"Probably not," Isabelle answered. "If that were the case, he would have taken his key back, by himself, a long time ago. No. He knew what it would take. He just needed to find the two of you."

CHAPTER 31

ONCE WE TURNED onto the main road a silence drifted over us. I'm sure that Sophie and Isabelle had each been somewhat traumatized by the events that unfolded tonight. The two of them seemed to quietly wrestle with their thoughts as we walked along. I thought it best to remain silent for now. This would give them some space and allow them to come to terms with their thoughts. The walk back to Isabelle's would be a quiet one. I felt relaxed and comforted knowing that none of us had been injured, that we now have the key, and all threats of danger had been removed.

The tranquil, serene beauty of our surroundings did not escape me along the way. The fields and forest on either side of us were lit up and shadowed by the moon above. A bright moonlit night allows us to see things in a different perspective. I wondered if this is how it always appears to the creatures of the night, a world void of color and yet clear as day.

As we approached Isabelle's house, I noticed a wagonload of hay parked next to it. It must have been from the livery next door. I looked at Sophie and asked, "Hey, how about right there tonight, instead of the little garlic room?"

A devilish grin came to her face as she said, "Under the stars and close to you... Makes me feel like we're back home."

I asked Isabelle, "Do you think we could borrow a couple of blankets, so that we might sleep out under the stars tonight," as I pointed to the wagon of hay.

"I think that could be arranged," Isabelle responded with an approving smile.

Sophie followed Isabelle into the house to help retrieve the blankets. She returned with three of them. "Isabelle said to put two blankets down beneath us to keep the hay from poking through."

"Sounds good to me," I said. Sophie and I climbed up on the wagon to spread out the first two blankets. We then cozied in together and covered ourselves with the third one.

The air was cool and fresh. There were no clouds in the sky, just a blanket of stars. It was a special night, for that large full moon also had a paraselene, a huge ring of light that circled the moon like a halo. "This was a great idea, Dawson. It looks so magical. We don't get this back home."

"I know. The city lights always seem to dull the view down."

"And I don't think I've ever seen a paraselene this wonderful. The moon is so huge and full, and that halo, so sharp and bright. Look how well defined those craters are on its surface. I'll bet the Watcher or the Elevator made this happen, just for us," Sophie laughed.

I glanced over, caught her eye, and winked at her. I was glad to see that she was enjoying this, and that her mind wasn't caught up in the events that happened earlier. Sophie snuggled in next to me. She softly said, "Dawson, tell me once more. Tell me what you see when you look up there. I like hearing it from you." She was tossing me one of her best dreamy-eyed looks.

I pondered for a moment, gazing at the wonder above. Then, speaking with a slow deliberate tone, I said, "When I look up there, I see a sapphire sky sprinkled with diamonds. I see the Earth and the Moon, locked in each other's grip, dancing across the heavens.

"You would be the Earth, and I would be the Moon. I circle around you every day, because I love to look at you. I face you always, never turning my back, ever attentive.

"I tug and stir your oceans, causing life to spring forth from you. And every night, I shine my love down on you."

Sophie leaned over and kissed my cheek. She whispered, "I love you," then nestled her face in against my shoulder.

As I gazed up at the heavens, I blocked everything else that happened this night from my mind, finding comfort from the beauty above and the beauty beside me. I drifted off to sleep with the alluring scent of her hair.

CHAPTER 32

SUNRISE ARRIVED MUCH too quickly for me. I found myself being tugged away from my dreams by the prodding voice of Isabelle.

"Dawson...Sophia, wake up. It's morning, and there's lots to do."

"Go away...You're popping my zzzzzz's," I replied.

"Come on you sleepyheads. I made you breakfast."

Sophie, without moving her head from my chest, mumbled, "Where does she find the energy?"

"I don't know, but breakfast sounds pretty good right now," I answered.

"Dawson, are you ever not hungry?" Sophie teased.

"Hey...I burn a lot of energy, and muscles need sustenance. So, if the foods ready, I'm ready. C'mon."

It felt as if we were on autopilot as we wearily climbed down and dragged our listless bodies toward the house. Still under the embrace of drowsiness, our minds seemed to lag a few feet behind our every step.

"Dawson, I sooo...need a cup of coffee right now," Sophie grumbled.

"No coffee. But, I do have a fresh pot of hot tea," Isabelle briskly replied.

I looked at Sophie and laughed, "She's awfully perky. She's probably already had three cups."

"Tea sounds just fine to me," Sophie answered.

As I walked through the front door, my senses instantly awakened to the mouthwatering aroma of bacon sizzling on the skillet. The three of us sat down at the table to a breakfast of pancakes and bacon, along with tea and cornbread.

After breakfast, Isabelle showed me how to use the ring to summon the Elevator. The silvery-gray ring had many strange symbols engraved along its band. A dark stone was mounted at the ring's center with two circular dials surrounding it. Each dial had numerous symbols engraved upon it and could be spun to the left or right to change the alignment of those symbols. Isabelle held the ring up and instructed me on how to turn the dials to properly align the symbols. She told me the stone would then begin to glow, summoning the Elevator.

We agreed that I would go back to the mansion to help Isaac with the clean-up process. Once finished, the Elevator could be called upon to return the captives to their homes. Sophie would remain here and help Isabelle until I returned.

I decided to leave the sword and backpack here at Isabelle's house. I removed four magazines of ammo and slid them into my coat pockets. Turning to Sophie with a longing look, I said, "I'll see you soon."

Sophie stepped over to me and placed her hand on my arm, saying, "I'm starting to miss you already." I reached out and took her into my arms. Holding her close, I gazed into her glossy eyes. I brushed her hair back and lightly stroked her cheek with my thumb. Without speaking, she mouthed, "I love you." I gave her a warm kiss good-bye. Then, I held her eyes in my gaze as I slipped out the door.

I didn't like the idea of being away from Sophie for a second time in this foreign place. However, she had been through enough already. I didn't want to expose her to the process of removing those dead bodies. Since the vampires were no longer around, she would be quite safe here with Isabelle.

CHAPTER 33

UPON REACHING THE mansion, I found Isaac and the others already at the task of removing the dead bodies. I joined them, providing assistance with carrying out some of the vampires and loading them upon the cart. Once we had loaded about ten to twelve bodies, the man up front cracked his whip. Instantly, the horse gave a tug and the cart began rolling on its way, out back and across the field. As we followed along on foot, I asked Isaac, "Where are we taking them?"

"We're giving them proper burials over by the edge of the field, where it butts up against the forest," he said.

"With the death of Voltaire, who now owns Graveswood Manor?"

"This house and land belonged to my family many generations ago, before Voltaire rudely took it away from us. We have lived on, as his servants ever since."

"Well, it looks as though it's back in the family again," I said. The thought pleased Isaac. This was evident from the quiet glow that lit up his face.

"I want to thank you, Mr. Dawson. Thank you for all that you have done."

"You played a vital role, Isaac. None of this would have happened if you hadn't steered us away from here and told us to seek out Isabelle."

"Ya know, I've known Isabelle my whole life. She was always very nice to me. I remember being drawn in by her beauty as a five year old. When I turned twenty-five, it seemed as if she hadn't aged a day. It's only recently that she's started to show her age. She knows all, and strangely, sometimes she knows things before they happen. She is quite a sweet and special lady."

I looked at him with a smile and said, "I can't argue with you there, Isaac. There's much more to your words than you know."

When we reached the point where the field and forest meet, I saw a number of men digging out shallow graves for each of the bodies. "Are all of these people, servants?" I asked.

"No, some of them are volunteers from the village," Isaac answered.

"Well, I commend you, Isaac. On such short notice you put the word out and organized all of this." I added, "You truly show the signs of a born leader."

We unloaded the bodies from the cart, slipping each into its own resting site, about three feet below the surface. Once the cart was empty, we turned and headed back for the next load. Meanwhile, the men with shovels took to the task of filling in the holes and digging new ones for the bodies yet to come.

While following the wagon back across the field, I said to Isaac, "I'll bet life is gonna seem more worthwhile around here, not being under the thumb of those vampires."

"That's a certainty. The shackles have been lifted. Once more, we will be free men, Mr. Dawson."

As we came around the front of the house we could see that Malcolm had a number of bodies out on the porch already, all lined up and ready to go. Isaac asked Malcolm, "What about the bodies from the third floor?"

"Yeah, I got that one too," Malcolm replied.

"What do you mean, one?" I asked. "There should be three bodies."

"There was only one body up there. It's this blond one over here," Malcolm answered.

It was Hanna that Malcolm was pointing to. I quickly scanned the other bodies lying on the porch, along with the few still remaining in the hall. Voltaire and Corin were not among them. Isaac and I looked at each other with a sense of urgency. The two of us started running toward the kitchen. I drew my gun and followed Isaac up the hidden staircase.

"Are you sure they weren't on any of the previous wagon loads?" I asked.

"I've seen every single body that has been loaded and unloaded to this point. So far, Voltaire and Corin have not been accounted for."

We entered the room and searched around, only to find it exactly as Malcolm had said. There were no other bodies, just blood stains where they had been. The tablecloth that Isabelle had covered Voltaire with was missing, along with one from another table.

"Two bodies and two tablecloths missing," I said. "I don't think Voltaire walked out of here. Someone wrapped each of them in a tablecloth and took them away. Do you think Malcolm had something to do with this?"

"No, not Malcolm. I'd find that hard to believe."

I stroked the stubble on my chin while I thought for a moment. I then mentioned to Isaac, "Voltaire's body would be too heavy for one man, for that matter, even Corin's when you consider that narrow staircase. Is there another way out of here?"

"Just the window," Isaac replied.

I leaned out the window and noticed an overhang above with a pulley attached for drawing large items up, but there was no rope running through it. Peering down at the ground below, I realized that it would be a long fall, and the grass down there looked undisturbed. I dreaded the thought, but had to ask, "If Voltaire's head came in contact with his neck could it possibly regenerate or mend itself, bringing him back to life?"

"I don't know," Isaac replied. "But, there is one other possibility. Voltaire's son may have come in during the night and recovered their bodies."

"Voltaire had a son? Why didn't anyone tell me?"

"He's not a part of the brethren here. He's sort of a renegade that lives in the wild."

"What's his name?"

"Ragnar," Isaac answered.

"Ragnar...What the hell kind of name is Ragnar?"

"It's a Viking name. It means fierce warrior."

"You're not making me feel comfortable, Isaac. Okay, I understand why he may have taken Voltaire. But why Corin? Unless..."

Isaac cut me off. "That's right, Mr. Dawson, Corin was his mother."

"This gets worse by the moment. All right, how did he get into the house last night, unnoticed?"

"We don't lock the doors. If he came in through the kitchen door, he could have gone up the stairs without anyone knowing."

Isaac's suggestion seemed quite plausible. Back in these days, I'm sure there were many people that didn't lock their doors, especially the inhabitants of this house. "Tell me about him," I insisted.

"Well, about twenty years ago Corin became Voltaire's wife. A year later, she gave birth to Ragnar. He is a full-blood. However, he's different, sort of an outcast by choice. Ragnar didn't like the fact that he was a vampire. He despised the other vampires and their way of life. He was a loner and found more comfort with the wolves in the forest, than the vampires here. One day he left, choosing a life with the wolf pack over one with the brethren."

It all made sense. That's why he wasn't present at the celebration. He loathed them all. On top of that, he probably wasn't too happy that his dad was marrying Hanna, in addition to his mother. He must have arrived much later, walking into the aftermath of the bloodshed. I could see it now. Ragnar claimed the two bodies that had meaning to him, his mother and father. He wrapped them in tablecloths and carried them down that little staircase by himself. I'm sure his strength was up to the task. Ragnar must have wanted to give them proper burials himself. In the back of my mind I still wondered if he was capable of bringing them back to life.

Then, there's that other issue...Vengeance. I'm sure his rage is building for whoever did this to his mother and father. He will be preoccupied at first with their burials or the healing process. As quick as he can though, Ragnar will be on the hunt for me.

CHAPTER 34

I KNEW THAT time was of the essence now. Once the sun settled over the horizon, darkness would come forth to unleash Ragnar. I said to Isaac, "Let's get back downstairs and finish this task, the sooner, the better." My main concern was to get back to Sophie and Isabelle as soon as I could.

Upon reaching the front door we saw that Malcolm, with the last of the bodies loaded on the cart, was already on his way out to the field.

"All right, Isaac," I said. "Now that the bodies are gone, we need to go downstairs and free the captives, so we can return them to their homes."

"But, Mr. Dawson, how will you get them home?"

I took the ring out of my pocket and placed it on my finger. I turned the dials as Isabelle had instructed. The ring grew warm and the stone began to glow. The ground around us started to shake and rumble. Directly in front of us, the dirt on the driveway began to open up as the Elevator majestically rose to the surface.

I looked at Isaac and couldn't help but laugh. He was totally dumbfounded. Isaac stood there, motionless, looking out over the top of his eyeglasses as they hung low on his nose. His eyes were wide open while his jaw hung halfway to the ground.

Finally, Isaac said, "I have heard the stories told, Mr. Dawson. But, never have I seen it for myself. I stand here staring with amazement while struggling to grasp its reality."

"Yeah, I know. It was a bit overwhelming for me the first time too."

The Elevator's door slowly opened. I stepped toward it with a bit of nervous apprehension. Then, I remembered what Isabelle had said, "Just talk to it. It knows you and will help you in any way that it can." I stepped inside and the door closed.

As I looked into the mirror I began to explain and unfold the events that had taken place. When I had gotten about halfway through the story, a notion came to me. You're finally seeing it for what it is, Dawson. None of this is necessary. The mirror knows it already. You were scanned upon entry. All the events that transpired were viewed through your mind.

I stopped talking for a moment while staring at my reflection. A voice then said, "You are correct in your assumption, Dawson."

"Then, why did you let me ramble on like that?"

"I saw something in you, earlier," The Elevator answered. "I put it to the test by dangling the image of a thought, hidden behind the mirror, to see if you could read it. You were tense and saw nothing at first. But, once you relaxed and allowed your mind to reach out, immediately, your eyes penetrated right through, grasping the notion I held, word for word."

"I don't recall seeing anything, other than my mirrored image. It was just a thought that came to me."

"That it did, word for word. You possess the talent. You just haven't figured out how to unlock its capabilities."

This conversation left me a little confused. I also got the feeling that the Elevator had decided to change the subject, for my mirrored reflection was now melting away as the mirror began fading to the color black. Slowly drifting toward the surface through the darkness, two deep blue eyes began to appear. They were huge, almost the size of tennis balls and sat further apart than human eyes. The eyes had round black pupils surrounded by an iris of deep ocean blue. The eyelids were boldly outlined in black. Surrounding each eye was a thin, whitish-gray shadow which gave the eyes a sort of mask like appearance. They seemed almost cat-like to me, not like an ordinary house cat, but like one of the big cats with their round pupils.

Instantly, the hair on the back of my neck stood up and a chill rolled down my spine as my imagination began to run wild. All I could think of is that I was being stared down by some giant tiger or leopard. Deep in my mind I knew that this wasn't the case and thus did my best to push those fears aside.

There was something about these huge eyes that made them powerfully hypnotic. My eyes seemed to be drawn in by them and try as I might, I couldn't look away. They also seemed to be a difficult read without a face around them. At one moment I felt as if they were menacing and yet in the next they seemed serene. These big eyes, being so close to me, pushed my senses to a heightened state of awareness. My eyes were wide open, and with each breathe I could feel my nostrils flaring.

In my mind, I methodically replayed back Isabelle's words about how he would help in any way that he can. Then, I asked those cat-like eyes if they could assist me in returning the captives to their homes.

"I know each of them. I shall return them to the exact place and time from whence they came," the voice responded.

"Thank you. Allow me to get them ready," I said. The Elevator door then slowly began to open.

Stepping out from the Elevator I noticed Isaac, over by the corner of the house, talking to three men. I recognized the three men as volunteers from the village who had assisted with the burial process. While walking toward them I began to wonder why the Elevator's presence hadn't drawn their attention. As I turned and looked back, I found my answer. The Elevator was totally invisible when viewed from this side. I let out a small chuckle of amusement. I knew it was still there. It was cloaking itself to remain out of their sight. That's absolutely incredible. This thing could be right next to you and you wouldn't even know it. I wish I had that kind of power.

I overheard Isaac say to the three men, "Did Malcolm not tell you of the risk you're taking? You should wait for us, and ride along in the coach."

The three men looked at each other, grumbling back and forth for a few seconds. Then, one of the men said, "We're not afraid. We'll be fine. Besides, we have our side-arms." He smiled with confidence while tapping his fingers on the pistol holstered at his waist.

"You're making a grave mistake. You don't know what's out there. You're taking your lives into your own hands," Isaac angrily responded.

One of the men rested a hand on Isaac's shoulder, saying, "Isaac, my friend. We'll meet you at the tavern. The first drink is on me." The three men then started walking down the driveway toward the road. Isaac wore a frown of frustration as he looked downward slowly turning his head from side to side.

I walked over to him, saying, "What's wrong? You seem troubled."

"Damn impatient fools," Isaac answered, as he viewed the three of them walking down the drive. "They should have waited for the coach." He then looked up at me, asking, "How did you make out with the Elevator? Will it deliver the captives back home?"

"All is ready. We just have to go down to the cellar and bring them up," I answered.

"Good. Let us hurry, and get this process rolling."

As we proceeded up the front stairs and through the wide open door, I stopped to give that large gargoyle knocker three heavy knocks. Isaac looked back at me with a foolish smile, saying, "The door is already open, Mr. Dawson."

"I know. I just had to do that," I said with a satisfying grin.

Isaac and I then brought up the captives, all twenty-eight of them, to the front hall. They were no longer in an entranced state. They were, however, afraid and confused. I spoke to them, saying, "The vampires have all been vanquished. All of you are free now, and we are beginning the process of returning you back to your homes."

The Elevator took seven individuals on its first trip. We watched as it disappeared, only to see it reappear three seconds later. Its door opened to reveal an empty Elevator. Isaac was astonished. "It just left. How could this be? Where did they all go?"

"Isaac," I said. "The Elevator time traveled into the future, delivering seven people to seven different places in time. Then, it probably stopped for a couple of brews before returning, three seconds after it left, just so it wouldn't bang into itself." I turned to the Elevator and shouted out, "Showoff."

Needless to say, the next three trips only took a couple of minutes. When finished, I told the Elevator I would summon it again, once Sophie and I were ready.

CHAPTER 35

ALL THAT WAS left to do now was bid farewell to Isaac. He was sitting on the steps watching as the Elevator disappeared for the final time. I stepped over to him, saying, "Isaac, it's time for me to head back to Isabelle's. The sooner that Sophie and I are out of this place, the better."

"I quite agree with you, Mr. Dawson. While you were talking to the Elevator, I instructed Malcolm to ready the coach and gather volunteers to ride along as protection. We will deliver you to Isabelle's."

"Well...I thank you. But, is that really necessary? It's the middle of the day. The sun is still strong in the sky. I'll be back to Isabelle's and gone before sunset. Sophie and I will be out of this world before Voltaire's son comes out to hunt."

"No, Mr. Dawson, you're mistaken. Remember I told you that Ragnar was different. Well, unlike the others, I've seen him out during the daylight hours. Somehow, his body has adjusted to the sunlight. He seems completely unaffected by it."

"Seriously... So, he could have been watching from the forest as we delivered the bodies to the burial site."

"I suppose. But, I wouldn't expect him to attack while we were providing proper burials for his own kind."

"Yeah. Ya got a point there. If he was watching, he was just putting a face on his enemy. Is this what you were talking about with those three men earlier?"

"Yes. It would not be safe for you to walk along that road back to Isabelle's. Malcolm is getting the coach ready as we speak. We shall bring guns and axes with us, just in case we encounter Ragnar. The coach should be ready to leave in about fifteen minutes. Give me a few moments to grab some things from inside the house. C'mon up and have a seat, and I'll be right back out." I followed Isaac up onto the porch. He went into the house while I settled into one of the rocking chairs.

Isaac was right. I'd be an easy target walking along that road by myself. I was glad I had brought those extra magazines of ammo. I wasn't sure what to expect from Ragnar. But, I knew that he would first and foremost be on the hunt for me. This gave me hope that Sophie and Isabelle were still okay.

As I relaxed in the rocking chair I began to picture those looks from Sophie's eyes earlier, first as I left her to follow Keos, once again on the third floor with the tear rolling down her cheek, and then once more as I was walking out the door at Isabelle's. These three images warmed my heart and brought a smile to my face. I spent a few moments savoring them, before tucking them away for another day. I then remembered what my mother used to say. "The mind is a treasure chest. Fill it with happy thoughts, visions of love, laughter, and good times. Reach in to them often, and you'll never, ever, find yourself alone."

CHAPTER 36

THERE'S NOTHING STEALTH about a horse and carriage. I could hear it approaching from out back long before it broke around the corner of the house. Something did seem different though. It was much louder than the coach that delivered Sophie and me yesterday. As it passed the corner of the house and came into view, I realized my ears weren't deceiving me. Malcolm was at the reins of a Concord stagecoach, similar to the one's Wells Fargo used during this era. It was drawn by two horses. He pulled the stage to a stop in front of the stairway. I recognized one of the horses as the same chestnut stallion that had brought us here. Along beside him now was a shiny black stallion.

Seated up front next to Malcolm was a man riding shotgun. I also noticed two men inside the coach peering out at me. At that moment the front door of the mansion opened and out walked Isaac wearing a tan cattleman's hat, a leather vest, and gloves. He held a shotgun under his left arm, nestled tight against his body. Isaac looked toward the coach as he shouted, "For those of you that don't know, this is Mr. Dawson."

Isaac then turned to me and introduced the others. "The man up there, next to Malcolm, is Edward. The two in the coach are Joseph on the left and Thomas to the right." We each exchanged a wave of the hand. Isaac next looked toward Malcolm, asking, "Does everyone have a gun?"

"Yes sir, three rifles and my shotgun," Malcolm replied.

"Would you like a rifle also, Mr. Dawson?" Isaac asked.

"Sure. Why not. You wouldn't happen to have a cannon, would you?"

Isaac laughed as he set his gun down against the doorway before going back into the house. He returned with a rifle in one hand, a bottle in the other, and a satchel hanging from his shoulder.

"What's the bottle for?" I asked.

Isaac tossed the rifle to me. "A sip of brandy for everyone," he replied. "It helps to take the nervous edge off."

"You won't get any argument from me," I muttered approvingly.

Isaac picked up his shotgun, and we started down the front steps. "What about axes?" Isaac asked, looking up at Malcolm.

"Two woodsman axes and this dragon slayer," Malcolm answered proudly, while hoisting up the largest medieval battle-axe I've ever seen. It had two half-moon blades, each about fifteen inches long, mounted on a four to five foot shaft. At the top of the axe handle a small spear tip protruded out between the blades. The size alone of this weapon would lead me to believe that one would need both hands to wield it.

"Where the hell did you find that?" Isaac asked.

"It was one of Voltaire's toys. He kept it in the barn."

Jokingly, I laughed up at him, "Malcolm, you are one crazy bastard."

"Yes I am," Malcolm replied. I could see he enjoyed the compliment, smiling from ear to ear as he placed the axe back down behind him.

"Say, Malcolm. Did Voltaire have any other war toys in the barn?" I asked.

"Yup. There's a stick that swings a chain with a spiked ball on the end. I think it's called a flail. There's also a mace, some battle hammers, a crossbow, and some daggers."

"Really." I looked at Isaac, saying, "I guess he liked medieval toys. We should take a quick run over to the barn before leaving."

"Malcolm, take us to the barn first," Isaac said, as we climbed aboard.

In two minutes time we were at the barn door. Malcolm slid it open and we followed him in. He led us to a small storage room with a padlock on the door. Malcolm reached up above the doorway, fishing around a bit with his hand before coming down with the key. He quickly removed the padlock and swung the door open.

Stepping in, we saw the items Malcolm had mentioned lying on a table. I picked up the flail and gently swung the spiked ball and chain. This weapon was fearsome looking, but seemed to lack any sense of control. If you swung it at your opponent and missed, there was a good chance you might whack yourself. I set it back down and began to admire the crossbow. This was a deadly weapon with incredible accuracy. There were four little arrows lying next to it. I remember Sophie called them bolts. I'm glad I paid attention when Sophie explained how crossbows work. I lifted it off the table and placed the nose of it against the ground. There was a stirrup built into its nose that I slid my foot into. It allowed me to use both hands to pull the bowstring back far enough to engage the lock. After picking up one of the bolts, I took the weapon out into the center aisle of the barn. Hanging on the far wall, about sixty feet away, was a metal pail. I placed the bolt into the groove on the crossbow, then took aim and fired. A loud clanging noise rang out as the bucket jumped off its nail and tumbled down to the floor.

"You seem to like that weapon," Malcolm said.

"That I do. It's incredibly accurate. It takes a lot of skill to shoot with a bow. This weapon already has the skill built into it. You just point and shoot."

"Yeah, but it takes a long time to reload between shots," said Malcolm.

"Then I'll have to make the first one count," I said, as we turned and headed back into the storage room. "Say, Malcolm. All these weapons look to be made out of forged steel. Are there any that are made out of silver?"

"Silver is too soft. When your weapons clash on the battlefield, you want yours to be made of the strongest metal. That would be steel," Malcolm answered. "But, if it's silver you're looking for, it's over here, right behind this curtain." Malcolm walked over to the edge of the room and drew back a curtain to reveal a closet with four shelves. Each shelf was filled with silverware, candle holders, drinking tankards and other silver items.

"So, that's where the fine silver went," barked Isaac. "It all disappeared long ago, only to be replaced by copper and tin items."

"Yeah. He removed it from the mansion and then hid the hoard in here," Malcolm said.

"How long have you known this?" Isaac asked.

"One night, a long time ago, I was up in the loft and spied Voltaire as he came into the barn. I watched as he reached up for the key and then entered the room. Later, and from time to time, I would enter the room. I would look, but not touch anything. I told no one. For if he found out, it would be my neck," Malcolm answered.

"What are these little domed things?" I asked.

"Those are sewing thimbles," Isaac answered.

"Oh yeah, like in the Monopoly game."

"What?" Isaac questioned.

"Never mind. They are made of silver. Correct?"

"Yes. One hundred percent solid silver," Isaac answered.

I picked up three of the thimbles and brought them to the weapons table. After placing a thimble over the arrowhead of one of the bolts, I hammered the tip of the arrow down twice against the table. The thimble was now tightly secured to the tip of the arrowhead. I repeated the process for the other two bolts. "Silver tipped arrows," I said. "Now, we should be all set to go." I picked up one of the daggers and slipped it under my belt. Isaac did the same. Edward seemed fascinated by the flail and decided to take that along.

Malcolm locked the storage room and closed the barn door behind us on the way out. I stopped by the side of the coach to set the crossbow one more time. Placing my foot in the stirrup, I pulled the bowstring up with both hands until it engaged the lock. Locked and ready to fire, I slid it under the seat in the coach along with the three bolts.

Isaac pulled out the bottle of brandy. He tossed it up to Malcolm and Edward, saying, "Just a couple of sips. We need you to stay sharp." Malcolm took a huge swig, then gave the bottle to Edward. Edward politely took a moderate sip and passed the bottle back. Malcolm, with a mischievous grin, couldn't resist taking one more hit from that bottle before popping the cork back in and tossing it down to Isaac. Once the rest of us had climbed aboard the stagecoach, Malcolm gave a crack of the whip, and we were on our way. Inside the coach, the four of us passed the brandy around twice before stowing it away.

"Isaac, tell me more about Ragnar. Did he get along with his father, and how does he compare in strength to Voltaire?" I asked.

Isaac pursed his lips together as he pondered for a moment. He then replied, "The two of them have completely different personalities. Voltaire was loud, bossy, and boastful. He was always in control. Things had to be done his way. No one dared to challenge him.

"Ragnar, on the other hand, was always observant, quietly surveying what was going on around him. He rarely spoke, unless it was to his mother or father. The other full-bloods seemed to cower in his presence. He showed them no fear, and also no respect. Ragnar had an obvious disdain for them.

"Ragnar is young, fast, and not one to mince words. As I said before, he doesn't like the fact that he's a vampire. He avoids the vampire way of life, choosing instead to live with the wolves in the forest. Ragnar's not one of those who would drink blood from your neck. Instead, he'd rather rip you apart and drink your blood while he's feasting on your insides.

"There was both a love and a respect between Ragnar and his mother and father. I think Voltaire and Corin longed for the day that Ragnar would return to live by their side."

For the next few minutes a silence seemed to settle over us. Each of us seemed to be preoccupied with our own thoughts as we peered out the windows of the coach.

I began to think about Sophie and how much I missed her. I could be in a room filled with people and find myself immersed in conversation, but the moment Sophie enters the room, she catches my eye. Sometimes I pretend not to notice. But I do see her every movement, each expression, and every fleeting glimpse her eyes take in my direction. She doesn't need to move her lips, for her eyes tell me everything I need to know. From across the room her glances tug at me, and I find myself drawn to her. Slowly, we drift toward each other through the crowd, tuning everyone else out along the way, until we reach each other and then there's only the two of us.

CHAPTER 37

WE WERE PROBABLY about halfway to the village when the carriage suddenly came to a stop. Isaac leaned out the window, yelling, "Malcolm, what's wrong? Why are we stopping?"

"There's a downed tree across the road, sir," Malcolm barked.

"Not by accident, I'm sure," I responded. "Anyone see any movement?"

A round of no's echoed from up front and next to me. "Well, it's a good thing you brought those woodsman axes. We'll have to get out and chop that tree up, so we can continue on," I said.

"Are you sure it's safe to get out right now?" Joseph nervously asked.

"Do you see anything out that window?" I questioned.

"No."

"Well, if we wait until it gets dark, do you think our odds are going to get any better?" I asked.

The doors opened and everyone began to climb down. "I think I see something on the other side of that downed tree," Edward yelled from up in the driver's seat.

We quickly grabbed our rifles and carefully proceeded forward, toward the tree blocking the road. As we grew closer, I saw what appeared to be a body lying on the other side of the tree. It was wrapped in a white tablecloth, similar to one of those missing from the third floor of the mansion. I leaped over the log and then nudged the covered body with the muzzle of my rifle. The body didn't move. I tried one more time, kicking it lightly with the side of my boot, still getting no response. I handed my rifle to Malcolm and drew my pistol. I didn't know what to expect. It could be Voltaire, Corin, or Ragnar lying in wait.

While pointing to Thomas and Joseph, I said, "Watch the forest on either side, so we're not caught off guard." I eyed the others, saying, "Keep your guns ready." Slowly reaching over with my left hand, I began to peel back the tablecloth.

Once I had pulled the cloth back far enough to reveal the head and face, I heard Isaac utter a sigh of sadness. "It's Riley Winston," he grumbled. I recognized Riley as one of the three men he had been talking to earlier, over by the corner of the house.

As I opened the tablecloth further, it revealed a horribly gruesome image. Riley Winston's body had been ripped wide open from his belt to his collar bone. Riley had also been disemboweled. Many of his organs were completely missing, while others looked chewed and strewn about. On his left side, some of his intestines were hanging out of the open wound, trailing down beside his body. His right arm was missing, viciously torn or gnawed off just above the elbow. Slowly, I peeled back the rest of the tablecloth to reveal his lower body. Riley's legs were intact, and his boots were still on. However, next to his legs were two other sets of boots, along with three pistols.

I covered Riley Winston's body back up with the tablecloth. As I stood up, I turned and scanned the perimeter, seeing only a stillness in the forest.

Looking toward the other men, I could see the fear written on their faces. I said, "Alright boys...It's Showtime. This is the spot he has chosen to do battle. The other two bodies are missing. He left this one as a message, to burn fear into your hearts and minds. It's his way of intimidating you. If you let him, or if you turn tail and run, you'll end up just like Riley. We need to stand tall and together as one. Voltaire and the rest of the vampires at the mansion have been vanquished. Now, we need to bring that same fate to Ragnar."

I had Malcolm bring the stagecoach forward, closer to the log. Meanwhile, Edward helped me move Riley Winston, wrapped in the tablecloth, off to the side of the road. I then instructed Joseph and Thomas to begin the task of chopping apart that tree. Isaac and Edward, with rifles in hand, walked back to the rear of the coach. Each stood guard at a corner, watching for any movement from the rear or respective sides. Malcolm and I did the same, up at the front of the horses. From there we could protect Joseph and Thomas while scanning the front, as well as the sides, for any movement. Joseph and Thomas nervously chopped away at the tree about twenty feet in front of us. Joseph was to the left, in front of Malcolm. Thomas was in front of me, on the right.

I noticed that the two of them spent half of their time looking at what they were cutting and the other half watching the forest for trouble. "You two should concern yourselves with making fast work of that tree," I said. "Malcolm and I will keep a lookout. We will protect you." From that point on they seemed a bit more focused, increasing their pace at chopping through the tree.

CHAPTER 38

To this point the horses had remained quite calm and relaxed. This seemed to be a good sign to me. I asked Malcolm, "How are these horses going to react to gunfire? Are they going to rear up and try to bolt?"

"No. They should be fine. I raised Cocoa, the chestnut stallion, since he was a little colt. Taught him not to fear the sound of a gun. I've hunted with him often. Numerous times, I've shot game from up in his saddle. Cocoa's as steady as they come. Noah is the black stallion. He's usually Isaac's ride. He too has been well trained. Noah's a year or two younger and generally follows Cocoa's lead when they're together."

That was a relief to hear. Trying to calm rampaging horses while fending off the opposition would only cause huge problems and weaken our line of defense. However, I also realized that Cocoa and Noah wouldn't react well to wolves. That's a predator vs. prey instinct that you can't take out of a horse. I looked toward the rear of the stagecoach and asked Edward, "All quiet back there?"

"No movement," he replied.

Joseph and Thomas had chopped about three quarters of the way through the tree when the horses began to act up. They both started snorting and flaring their nostrils. Cocoa raised and lowered his head. Noah began to shuffle about on his hooves. I knew they had a much finer tuned sense of smell and hearing than the rest of us. "Be sharp everybody. We have company," I said. I kept the rifle nestled against my shoulder as I looked down the barrel, scanning the forest.

Suddenly, out of the corner of my eye, I saw a large gray wolf bolt out from the trees and leap toward Thomas. I turned and fired, barely able to take aim. The wolf tumbled to the ground. Thomas and Joseph dropped their axes and ran, screaming like a couple of school girls, back between Malcolm and me to the front of the horses. Now, the howling of wolves began to echo throughout the forest.

"You two left your guns on the ground by the log," I shouted to Joseph and Thomas. They looked at me with terror on their faces. "You can't defend yourselves without your guns. We'll cover you. Go get them," I said.

Joseph and Thomas briefly looked at each other without saying a word, their faces filled with distress. Swiftly, they turned and raced out to the fallen tree to grab their rifles. As they scurried back, all hell broke loose.

Wolves charged out at us from the forest. Gunfire erupted from all sides of the stagecoach. I yelled to Thomas and Joseph to fall back on each side and cover the middle of the coach. They did so, while Malcolm and I covered either side of the horses. It seemed like every few seconds another wolf would come charging out at me from the cover of the trees and bush, snarling with huge fangs. Some of the wolves were black, a few were white, but most of them wore a coat of gray. These wolves looked massive, probably somewhere upwards of a hundred and fifty pounds each. Sometimes they attacked in pairs, which barely gave me time to get a second shot off.

Once, I missed on my second shot and the wolf, while in mid-air, latched his teeth down on the barrel of my rifle. I pulled the dagger from my belt and stuffed it into his ribcage as he crashed up against me. His body went limp, and he crumpled to the ground.

Off to my right, out of the corner of my eye, I saw a large black wolf break through and lunge at Thomas. The wolf caught Thomas in the left shoulder, driving him backwards, crashing up against the carriage. With no time to aim, I spun around and fired my rifle. The wolf let out a yelp and crumpled to the ground. Thomas staggered to the right a step or two, struggling to regain his balance against the side of the carriage, before collapsing to the ground himself.

CHAPTER 39

SHORTLY AFTER THOMAS went down the wolves stopped charging out at us. The gunfire suddenly came to a halt, but my ears were still ringing. It appeared as though the first wave of their assault was over, at least for the moment anyway.

I raced toward Thomas, as did Edward from the rear of the coach. Thomas was alive, but looked to be in a state of shock or confusion. It appeared as though his head and neck were untouched, but his shoulder was mangled and bloody.

"Edward, drag him under the carriage. Tear his shirt off. Use some of it to pack against the wound. Use the rest of it to bandage his shoulder. Keep it snug." I then yelled, "Is everyone on that side of the carriage okay?"

"Yes sir, Mr. Dawson," Isaac said.

I turned, scanning the forest on our side once more. There was no movement and no sounds, only a dead stillness.

"Dawson...We got trouble," Malcolm yelled from the other side of the coach. "The wolves are getting up."

I couldn't believe what I was hearing. I climbed up the side of the carriage and stood on its roof to get a better view. Malcolm was right. We had dropped these wolves with rifles, but now they were rising and moving off. I rolled my eyes and slowly blew out a long breath of frustration. It was a disturbing thought. But somewhere along the way, Ragnar must have been mixing his blood with that of these wolves.

I dropped my rifle and quickly ran forward to grab the battle-axe from behind the driver's seat. "Malcolm," I yelled. "Slice 'em wide open," I added, as I tossed the battle-axe down to him. I then drew my pistol from its holster and began firing at every wolf I saw rising. One silver bullet for each of them. Each time I emptied a magazine, I popped it out and slid a full one in. I saw Malcolm down below, on the other side, running from one wolf to the next, swinging that mighty battle-axe and tearing open their bodies.

All of this suddenly came to a dead stop with the thunderous howl of another wolf. Only, we all knew this wasn't a wolf. The howling sound came from up front. As I turned, looking forward from the roof of the stagecoach, I saw Ragnar. He was standing there, in the road, about fifty yards in front of the horses.

"Edward, quickly, hand me that crossbow in the carriage," I said. Edward swiftly opened the door and jumped aboard the carriage. Without delay he reached up and slid the crossbow along with two darts up onto the roof. I knelt down slightly, picking up the crossbow without taking my eyes off of Ragnar.

Even from this distance, I could tell he was Voltaire's son. Ragnar was tall, lean, and ripped with muscles. His dark curly hair hung down to his shoulders. He wore no shirt or shoes, only a pair of pants that had the legs torn off above his knees.

Ragnar extended his arm forward, pointing toward me, and yelled, "Daw...son!" He broke into a sprint, straight down the road toward me. I loaded a bolt into the crossbow and took aim. He was fast and closed the distance quickly. I heard the guns from below firing at him, but he neither flinched nor broke stride. I aimed for the center of his chest and took my shot. The bolt struck him in his left shoulder. His shoulder kicked back slightly, but Ragnar didn't slow down.

Ragnar hit the log in front of us and vaulted forward, over Cocoa's head. He touched down with one foot onto the horse's back and leaped right up to the driver's seat of the coach. He stopped for a moment and stood straight up. His rifle wounds were closing up now. Ragnar reached up and grabbed the arrow sticking out of his shoulder. With a grimace he ripped it out and tossed it to the ground below. My hope was that the silver thimble may have dislodged from the arrowhead and now remained inside his body.

Ragnar stood there, staring at me with a grin that spoke of bold confidence. He had those same steel gray eyes as his father. He was toying with me for a moment, much like a predator with its prey cornered, before closing in for the kill.

Slowly, Ragnar took one more step up onto the roof. I raised my pistol as he began walking toward me. I fired five shots, circling his chest and gut, trying to spread the liquid silver throughout. Those earlier rifle shots that struck Ragnar never fazed him, but now I could see his face contorting from the agony. He clinched his fists trying to fight off the pain as his body began to slump forward. He stood there, hunched over, right in front of me.

Ragnar then caught me off guard. With lightning speed he swung his left arm upward, backhanding the pistol out of my hand. The pistol bounced across the roof and tumbled over the edge to the ground below. Ragnar gritted his teeth as he fought off the pain and forced himself to straighten back up. A black ooze began to trickle out from his arrow and pistol wounds.

I reached for the dagger tucked under my belt and came up empty. I now remembered that I left it in the wolf down below. I was without a weapon.

I swung with my right fist, catching Ragnar in the jaw. That was a mistake. It was as if I had punched a stone statue. My knuckles ripped open with the impact, while his jaw never budged. It was my turn to grit my teeth as I dragged my right arm up and down trying to shake loose the stinging pain in my hand.

Ragnar reached back with his right and launched a haymaker at me. He didn't swing with a fist. Instead, he swung with an open hand, much like a bear or cat would with its paw. It came from down low, arcing diagonally upward. I leaned back trying to avoid the blow. He caught me with those nails, or claws of his, slicing upward through my coat. I felt the burn as they reached deep enough to slice through my skin. The force of the blow lifted me off my feet and launched me over the back side of the coach. I felt as if I was falling in slow motion as I twisted my body in mid-air trying to regain my balance. Like a fallen tree my body slammed to the ground hard, raising a cloud of dust all around me.

Every bone in my body ached. My chest throbbed with a stinging pain from where his claws had ripped through my skin. My head was spinning and my mind was disorientated. Fortunately, I didn't feel as if I had any broken bones. I pushed myself up on one elbow and spit the dirt out of my mouth. I shook my head back and forth trying to clear away that groggy feeling. At that moment, I spied my pistol on the ground about fifteen to twenty feet in front of me. While still struggling to get a grip of my faculties, I began crawling toward my gun.

I was probably about five feet from my gun when I saw Ragnar's feet slam to the ground on either side of me. My eyes opened wide as I muttered, "Not good." Suddenly, I felt his hand reach in by the back of my neck as he grabbed a hold of my coat collar. He lifted me up with one hand and tossed me back toward the coach like a rag doll. The back of my body took the impact as I slammed up against the coach. My body then crumpled to the ground below.

While on the ground I noticed Isaac step out from behind the rear of the coach and launch his dagger at Ragnar. The dagger struck deep into Ragnar's thigh. Ragnar just growled and pulled the dagger out of his leg. Isaac turned and ran behind the carriage as Ragnar wound up to throw the dagger back. There was a loud thwack as the dagger struck the rear of the coach where Isaac had been only a moment before. That's when I decided to roll out of the way for a moment, beneath the carriage, to buy some time.

While rolling underneath the carriage I bumped into Thomas. I brushed some of the dirt off me and said, "Hey Thomas. What's up? How's that shoulder doing?"

A look of sheer terror came over Thomas's face as he said, "Are you crazy? You're gonna bring him under here."

With a chuckle, I replied, "There's nothing to fear. I've got him on the run."

"The only running he's doing, is after you," said Thomas. Suddenly, I saw that look of terror come back to Thomas's face.

He couldn't find the words. He just raised his hand and pointed to his left.

With a turn of my head, I saw Ragnar bending over and peering underneath the carriage at us. Turning back to Thomas, I gave him a slap on his good shoulder and said, "Catch ya later." Quickly, I rolled out from under the carriage, off to the other side, away from Ragnar. After getting to my feet, I began to climb up the side of the coach, back to the roof once more.

Upon reaching the roof, I heard Isaac yell, "Dawson." As I looked down to him, Isaac tossed his shotgun up to me.

Catching the gun, I yelled back down to him, "I need my pistol."

Isaac looked at me as if I had lost my mind, saying, "A shotgun is much better than a pistol."

"Not this tiii..me," I said with an urgency.

From behind me I heard a solid thud hit the roof. Turning around quickly, I saw it was Ragnar. He had vaulted up to the roof from the ground below. He stood there on the other side of the roof, about ten to twelve feet in front of me, wearing that cocky smile of his. We glared at each other for a second or two. Then, I heard a chain rattling down below to the right. Looking down, I saw Edward swinging that stick with the spiked ball and chain over his head, like a cowboy with a lasso. My eyes opened wide as I muttered to myself, "Oh no. This can't be good."

"Don't worry, Dawson," shouted Edward. "I got him in my sights."

"Yeah, that's what I'm afraid of," I muttered again.

Edward released the flail casting it upward in the direction of Ragnar. Only, it wasn't heading toward Ragnar. It was sailing straight up toward me.

I ducked my head quickly, yelling, "Holy shit," as the spiked ball and chain whistled past my ear. Straightening back up, I looked down at Edward with a less than happy face. "What the hhhell was that?" I barked.

Edward looked at me like a little kid who just broke a window with a baseball. "Sorry," he responded.

Out of the corner of my eye I noticed Ragnar coming toward me. He was roughly three feet away from me when I fired the shotgun at his stomach. The force of the impact knocked him back a couple of steps. Ragnar now had a two inch hole through his gut. Light from the other side of his body was visible through the opening. Ragnar caught his balance and straightened back up. While still looking at me with that obnoxious grin, he slowly shook his head from side to side – No. With catlike speed he reached out and snatched the shotgun from my hands. Ragnar then tossed it back over his shoulder like a toy. That huge hole through his stomach was now quickly closing back up. Only the arrow and pistol wounds remained open, still continuing to ooze blood.

Ragnar reached out and grabbed me by the upper arms. Slowly, he lifted me up in front of him. Meanwhile, over his shoulder I happened to notice Malcolm climbing up to the roof from the driver's seat.

Looking for a way to distract him and buy some extra time, I asked Ragnar, "Why is it that sunlight seems to have no effect on you, while all the others avoid it like the plague?"

"It has evolved from years of crossing my blood with that of hundreds of wolves."

"Yeah, I noticed the wolves benefited from that too."

Ragnar didn't reply. Suddenly, his eyes shot wide open. He was looking at me, but seemed to be in a daze. I saw his nose twitch, sniffing the air twice. I realized he must have picked up the scent of my bloody knuckle. Ragnar's eyes took on a menacing glow. He glared at me sternly, saying, "No more talk." Ragnar began squeezing harder on my arms. He snarled at me, showing his teeth and fangs. I knew that any moment now, those fangs would tear into me.

I gritted my teeth, thinking, *Not now, Not here.* Quickly, I drew my knees up to my chest as I muttered, "Hungry? Eat my Timberlands, dogbreath." Kicking as hard as I could, I shot the soles of my boots right into his jaw. The force of the blow knocked his head back. His lip was split open and oozing blood. Ragnar grew enraged. He opened his mouth wide, releasing a loud throaty growl like that of a mountain lion.

Over his shoulder, I saw Malcolm raise up the battle-axe from behind. He swung it over the top, bringing it down with all his might into the middle of Ragnar's back. Ragnar lurched forward from the force of the blow.

The battle-axe blade pierced right through and out the front of Ragnar's chest. Ragnar and I both gazed down at this shiny axe-blade protruding out from his chest, a good two to three inches. That same black ooze I had seen with Voltaire began to trickle out along the blade, dripping down to the roof of the coach below. Liquid silver from the pistol shots was also seeping out with it.

Ragnar released me, and I fell backward to the roof of the coach. I looked up to see him tighten his fists and clench his teeth as he fought to straighten up his body. Ragnar's speed was considerably compromised at this point. Angrily, he turned around to face Malcolm. Malcolm instantly turned white as a ghost and began backpedaling. Ragnar swung his arm wildly, trying to catch Malcolm. He would have connected if Malcolm hadn't tripped over the crossbow and tumbled backward onto the driver's seat. Ragnar slowly started walking toward Malcolm.

I quickly jumped to my feet and then grabbed the handle of the battle-axe. Ragnar could feel my grip right through its blade. He immediately stopped in his tracks. I rocked the handle hard to the left and then back to the right. This would loosen up the blade while inflicting more pain and damage inside. I gripped the handle tightly with both hands and then forcefully ripped the axe out of his back. Ragnar arched backward and howled to the sky in agony.

Ragnar furiously turned back around to me again. He started to raise his right arm as if to strike a blow. Quickly, I raised the axe up and out to the side as I spun around backwards on one foot. I then planted my other foot and swung with the battle-axe as hard as I could. I caught Ragnar on his left side, just below his ribs. The axe sliced right through his body with no resistance.

A look of shock came over his face. Ragnar's mouth hung open, and his eyes remained fixed on me as his upper body slowly slid off the lower half and tumbled over the side of the coach. His lower body stood there for a few seconds, spasmodically twitching, before collapsing into a heap.

CHAPTER 40

A BLANKET OF unruffled silence, much like that which accompanies a softly falling snow, now seemed to consume the forest. It was as if time had stood still. Every living thing seemed frozen in place, stunned by what had just happened. I was still caught up in the adrenaline rush. My hands were locked in a tight grip of the battle-axe while Ragnar's blood continued to drip from its blades. All I could do was stand there, staring at Ragnar's lower half, waiting for it to get back up.

A few moments passed before I finally snapped out of it. Dropping the axe, I made my way forward to Malcolm. He was lying on his back, across the driver's seat. When his eyes caught mine a smile came to his face.

"Malcolm," I said with a smile. "When I first met you, I thought you were a crazy lunatic. Now...I'm sure of it." Malcolm burst into laughter. Reaching down with my hand, I caught his and hoisted him to his feet.

"Thank you, Dawson. You saved my life."

"No, Malcolm. I think it was quite the opposite."

"Either way, we make a good team. Don't we?"

"That, we do," I answered.

I was proud of Malcolm. I remembered what my dad used to tell my brother and me when we were younger. "If you must go into battle, don't lose your wits. You need to stay sharp, move fast, and have more grit and stones than your enemy."

Today, we found ourselves up against a far superior warrior, in Ragnar. Malcolm could have stood frozen with fear, or run off into the woods. Instead, he showed some grit and stones. Call us lucky if you wish. But on this day, together we forged a path to victory.

Voices from below meant the others had begun to stir. Malcolm and I climbed down to check on the condition of Thomas, along with Ragnar's upper half. Thomas was no longer under the carriage. Edward had bandaged him well, keeping his blood loss to a minimum. Thomas was now standing beside the coach with the others, viewing what was left of Ragnar. Thick, black, foamy blood oozed out of Ragnar's lifeless upper body as it lied there, face down, on the ground next to the carriage.

"We must have a drink to celebrate our victory," Isaac shouted before he climbed into the coach to retrieve the bottle of brandy. I was beginning to notice that there was definitely some similarities between these guys and my friends back home.

"The injured get first dibs," Thomas yelled. It appeared as though Thomas had now fully regained his composure.

"You need medical attention. We need to get you to a doctor," I said.

"All in good time. Right now, we need to celebrate," he said, raising the bottle to his lips.

It could be that his condition was not as serious as I previously thought. It could also be that he just loves the alcohol. The more I thought about it, the more I realized that back in these days alcohol was probably the anesthetic a doctor would use before performing surgery. I suppose that Thomas was just getting himself a head start on his anesthesia.

"There's a doctor in the village. He should be fine until we get there," Isaac said.

The bottle passed from one hand to the next, with each of us taking a hit as it made the rounds, until we drank it dry. The brandy seemed to calm and relax me, removing those edgy feelings left over from the battle with Ragnar.

With the bottle now empty, and knowing that we still had work to get done, Joseph and I took to the task of removing that tree that blocked the road. Meanwhile, Edward and Malcolm unstrapped shovels from the side of the stagecoach to dig a grave for Ragnar. The work was easier now, without having the stress of a possible attack looming over one's shoulder.

When Joseph and I finished cutting through the tree, we rolled it off to the side of the road. Next, we lifted the body of Riley Winston, wrapped in its tablecloth, and loaded it onto the carriage. By this time, Malcolm and Edward had finished digging a shallow grave for Ragnar. Malcolm and I slipped Ragnar's upper and lower body halves down into the hole. Then Edward and Joseph, with shovels in hand, took to the task of covering him up. While they did, I helped Isaac gather all the weapons and load them aboard the coach. I searched and found both the dagger I had used on the wolf along with the bolt Ragnar had ripped from his shoulder and tossed to the ground. I placed them under the seat next to the crossbow.

With our work done here, we climbed aboard the coach and continued on our way to the village. Thomas was now beginning to look a bit pale, but he wasn't complaining. Maybe the brandy had helped take the edge off his pain. Quietly, he sat there deep in thought, probably mulling over what the doctor would need to do.

CHAPTER 41

MALCOLM GOT US to the village in no time at all. He pulled the stagecoach right up to the front of the doctor's house. Amidst all the commotion, the doctor came running out to see what had happened. Isaac immediately began to inform the doctor of the events that led to the injury while the other men helped Thomas into the house.

Once inside, the doctor had Thomas lie down on a table. The doctor removed the bandage and began to examine the wound. After a few minutes of gentle poking and prodding, he said, "Thomas is a lucky man. His arteries were untouched. He has suffered some tissue, ligament, and muscle damage. I'll clean his wound and sew what I can back together. It may take weeks, even months, to fully heal. Barring infection, he should make a full recovery. Of course, there's always that possibility that he may lose some range of motion."

We often tend to fear the worst in situations like this. The doctor's prognosis was encouraging. As a result, we all breathed a sigh of relief. "I'll get started right away," the doctor said. "Joseph, you have helped me once before. Will you be able to assist me?"

"Yes sir. Of course," Joseph replied. The rest of us then filed out of the room so that the doctor could get started.

Outside, I thanked the others and bid my good-byes. Turning to Malcolm, I smiled and said, "Malcolm, yesterday, I thought you were a strange and a rather odd character. Today, I saw the real you." With a smirk, I said, "You're even more strange and odd than I thought." This brought a big smile to his face.

With a more serious tone, I said, "All kidding aside, we do make a great team. No matter how difficult the confrontation, I know that we would have each other's back covered."

"Thank you, Dawson. Coming from you, that's a compliment. I consider myself lucky, and a better man for knowing you." The two of us then shook hands.

I next turned to Edward. He immediately said, "I'm sorry, Dawson."

"Think nothing of it, Edward. That weapon is incredibly difficult to control. You missed me, and that's what matters most. Your intentions were good, and at least you had the stones to give it a shot. You didn't run and hide. You stood up and fought when it counted. I'm proud of you, for the courage you brought to the battle."

"Thank you, Dawson. I'll never forget you," Edward proudly replied.

Next, I turned to Isaac. He looked at me and asked, "Don't you think the doc should have a look at your chest?"

"I'll be fine. I'm kinda used to getting clawed open. What about Riley?" I asked.

"It's time for you to go home. We'll take care of Riley." Isaac answered.

"You're a true friend, Isaac. Without you, the outcome would have been much different. You went way out on the limb for a couple of strangers. I know you took some huge risks in doing so. I want to thank you for that. I'm very happy the mansion is back in the hands of your family. With your leadership skills, you'll have no problems running it."

"Mr. Dawson, we are all in your debt. We are all free again, thanks to you. You have become a hero to the other men. I can only hope that your courageous approach has worn off on them. I'm sure it will have a positive effect on each of them going forward." Isaac reached into his satchel and pulled out a bottle of wine. "Here, take this for you and Sophia, from me. I wish you a safe journey."

"Thank you, Isaac. That reminds me. I almost forgot." I opened the carriage door and retrieved the crossbow and dagger, along with the three bolts, from under the seat. "Oh...By the way, Isaac. If by chance this territory should develop a problem with wolves that are more than what they seem, make sure your bullets are made of silver." I shook his hand, waved goodbye to the others, and started walking in the direction of Isabelle's house.

CHAPTER 42

W HILE CROSSING THE center of the village, I stopped at the well to rinse some of the battle off my face and hands. After drawing up a full bucket of water, I cupped my hands, dipped them in, and splashed my face and neck a number of times. With wet hands I wiped down the front of my coat, before leaning forward and pouring the rest of the water through my hair.

Yeah. That water was really cold, forcing a few deep breaths from me. I shook my head a couple of times and then briskly ruffled my hair with my fingertips, flicking away the excess water. Now, at least, I looked a little more presentable.

When I reached Isabelle's I leaned the crossbow up against the house between the wood pile and the front door. After two quick knocks, Sophie opened the door for me. She didn't have to say a word. The look on her face was one of relief. She must have been worrying while I was away. Her nervous expression quickly melted away. She now wore a tender smile along with a soft seductive glow in her eyes. It warmed my heart to see her face again. I leaned forward and kissed her. "Hi, sweetie. Look what I have. It's a present from Isaac."

"Ohh...That was nice of him." She took the bottle from me and brought it over to the table. Stepping in and closing the door, I noticed a young girl, maybe in her late teens, seated at the table. I did not, however, see any sign of Isabelle.

As I approached the table, Sophie turned to me and said, "Dawson, your breath smells like alcohol, your coat is ripped, and what on earth happened to your hand?" With a painful expression on her face, she picked up my hand and began to examine my knuckles. "You were drinking and got into a fight. Didn't you?"

"I got into a fight and then had a drink. There is a difference." Her eyes narrowed as she scolded me with her stare. "I didn't start it, babe."

"But, you still got into it."

"It wasn't my fault," I said, while glancing toward the young girl seated at the table.

Sophie took a clean cloth and dipped it into a pan of water on the counter. After wringing the water out, she gently wrapped the cloth around my knuckles. Her touch was soft and soothing. That warm glow had returned to her eyes. I found myself smiling. With a soft tone, she said, "Dawson, that's not what you left here to do."

"I know. I didn't have a choice."

"Dawson, there's always a choice. You should have walked away."

"You don't understand."

"Yeah...Someone else started a fight, and you got into it. You know that two wrongs don't make a right."

"Yeah...Well, how about two lefts and then a right?"

She did her best to fight off a smile while giving me the eyebrows again. She then asked, "And did anyone else get hurt?"

"One guy with a mangled shoulder, and one that's only half of what he used to be." Sophie stared at me with a confused look on her face. "Where's Isabelle?" I asked.

"She stepped out for a moment. Good news travels fast. It appears as though you and I are the talk of the village today. This young girl is one of Isabelle's neighbors. She baked an apple pie for us." My eyes lit up when Sophie mentioned apple pie. Sophie brought the pie from the counter to the table.

As I sat down, the neighbor girl got up and went to the cupboard for plates, silverware, and glasses. I did my best to feign a disinterest. However, one would have to be a blind man not to notice how strikingly beautiful she was as she went about setting the table for us.

"We should wait for Isabelle's return before we begin slicing the pie," I said to Sophie.

"Of course," she replied, smiling back at me as she sat down. "So, how did you make out with your other chores, up the road?" I could tell by the way she phrased the question, that I should be careful what I say in front of this young neighbor girl.

"I helped Isaac and the others clean everything up. The ring worked like a charm, exactly as Isabelle said it would. Then, all the displaced people were ferried back home." I noticed that Sophie was still looking at me with a grin. This led me to wonder if I had slipped and said something wrong.

Across the table from me, the young girl quietly slipped back into her chair. I reached for the bottle of wine, saying, "I don't think Isabelle will mind if we crack open the wine while we wait." I poured myself a glass and raised it to my lips. As I took a sip, my eyes caught the young girl watching me. Placing my glass down, I thought, *She's absolutely gorgeous. But there's something else, something strange about the way she looks at me. It's almost the same way as...*

"That's right, Dawson," she said.

I fell over backwards in my chair. The voice was Isabelle's. I jumped back up, with my mouth and eyes wide open, staring in disbelief. All the while, the two girls roared with laughter. It all became clear to me now. Under the tablecloth she had collected Voltaire's blood in those bottles.

"So...How do I look, Dawson?"

"You look... stunning. I can see why Voltaire had such a fascination and desire for you." I then realized that what I said might get misconstrued. Glancing Sophie's way, I noticed that her eyeballs had begun to resemble daggers.

I turned back to Isabelle with a smirk, saying, "You know what. You and Sophie are very much alike. Sophie has a kind of magnetic allure that tenderly tugs on me and draws me in. I'll bet that you had that same effect on Voltaire."

I glanced Sophie's way once more and noticed things were looking much better now. The eyeballs no longer resembled daggers. A smile had come over her face, and she began to wave at me. I know it was only one finger, but at least she was waving.

CHAPTER 43

MY MOUTH WAS watering. The sight and smell of that fresh baked apple pie had teased me for long enough. My mind decided to take a back seat now, surrendering all control to the urges of my stomach. After all, we didn't have to wait any longer, for Isabelle was already here. Once I righted my chair I sat back down, focusing first on slicing a big piece of pie for myself. With this most important matter out of the way, I proceeded to ask Isabelle, "So, tell me. How did you make this happen?"

"Well, while you were gone..."

That's all I heard. I thought I could dive into this pie while listening to her story. Not a chance. With the very first bite, I drifted off to heaven. My taste buds were celebrating the crisp savory texture and juicy flavor of the apples. They were sugary-sweet with just a hint of tartness, and covered with a warm cinnamon and brown sugar glaze that had my mouth begging for more. The golden crust was flaky, warm, and tender. Each bite seemed to melt in my mouth. Homemade from scratch, you just can't get any better than that.

Damn... I suddenly realized that I had zoned out and wasn't paying attention. Maybe they didn't notice. I looked toward Sophie. She had a big smirk on her face. No fooling her. She knows me too well. She read me like a book.

I quickly turned back to Isabelle, who had stopped talking moments earlier. She was staring at me now, with a stern look on her face. Busted...Forget the book, she read my mind. I then thought to myself, *Sorry, I got distracted by the pie you made. It's incredibly good.*

A big smile came over Isabelle's face as she looked back at me. She turned to Sophie and laughed as she said, "He takes down a whole houseful of vampires, and then falls victim to a piece of pie." The two of them giggled with amusement.

"Alright, I'm sorry. Start over. I'll pay attention this time," I said.

Isabelle, still chuckling behind that smile, said, "Well, while you were gone I showed Sophia how it works. It only takes a small sip of Voltaire's blood to peel back the years and return my body to its prime youthful state."

I swallowed the bite of pie I was working on and said, "The results are amazing, but how long does it last? I mean, before it wears off?"

"It doesn't wear off at all. Once I've rejuvenated back to my prime, I begin the process of aging again at the same pace as everyone else."

"Really. Well, for your own safety, try not to let anyone else know about this. There are people and governments that would target you and exploit this for their own gain. That aside, enjoy yourself. With the supply you have, you could be around for a lot of lifetimes."

"That depends on your frame of mind. At some point I'll give up cheating time. It's not easy starting over while everyone that you've loved or known has either passed away, or are in their final years."

"Well, since you're starting over again, why don't you come back home with us. We'll help you settle in and start a new life."

"Sophia made that same offer earlier, and we discussed it at length. No, Dawson. I've seen the future through your eyes. It's too fast, too congested, and way too confusing. Sophia and I came up with a better plan. All you need to do now is finish that last bite of pie and summon the Elevator."

I did so, placing the ring on my finger and spinning the dials until they were aligned properly. Once again, the stone began to glow. I picked up the backpack, along with the bottle of wine. Isabelle took a small satchel from the counter with her. I took one last look around the room and said, "What about all this other stuff. Are you just going to leave it?"

"I have no use for it," Isabelle replied.

I picked up the small paddle I had used for the loaf of bread earlier. "I kinda like this." I looked toward Sophie with a raised eyebrow and said, "Maybe we could find a use for this."

"Absolutely not," she replied.

"But, what if we find a boat?" I laughed.

"Yeah. Nice try, Dawson."

"Ahh Sophie, where's your sense of adventure?"

"Dawson, haven't you had enough adventure for one weekend?" she scolded.

"Oh...Alright," I said reluctantly, as I set the paddle back down. I then reached out and took Sophie by the arm and whispered, "By the way, I got you a present."

"You did," she said with surprise.

"It's just outside the door."

Sophie was full of excitement and scooted out the door just ahead of Isabelle and me. Catching sight of the crossbow, she shouted, "Dawson, this is over five hundred years old and yet it looks brand new! Where did you find it?"

"Do you like it?"

"I love it!" She jumped into my arms and gave me a big hug. She then whispered in my ear, "You have no clue what that's worth. Do you?"

"Nope."

"Where did you get it?"

"Voltaire kept a stash of medieval toys in the barn. I knew you'd like this one."

Sophie kissed my cheek and whispered, "Thank you."

After sliding the three bolts into her boot, she picked up the crossbow. The three of us then headed around to the backside of the house where the Elevator was surfacing.

CHAPTER 44

UPON ENTERING THE Elevator, Isabelle immediately began to focus her gaze upon the mirrored wall. The mirror quickly responded by fading to black. Then those huge cat-like eyes reappeared once more as the voice spoke to Isabelle. "It's a pleasure to see you again. Time has passed, but somehow, you look remarkably the same."

"Thank you."

"I have a message for you."

"You do?"

"Yes. I've just returned from the Watcher. I had a question that I knew only he could answer. His words to me were as follows. 'You, my wisest of heralds, have served me well. I knew you would find a resolution to this matter without becoming directly involved. I also know you stand before me seeking an answer to something you stumbled upon. Bring back this message to Isabelle from me. Within, lies your answer.'"

Out of the darkness below those cat-like eyes came a spiral of hundreds of little starry lights. They swirled around for a moment before gelling together to spell out a message.

Blood of your blood.
Had you fallen in battle,
Instantly, so would have he.
Live long, Isabelle,
And forge a path for him.

Once Isabelle finished reading the message the words faded into darkness. "I'm confused," Isabelle said. "I don't quite understand the Watcher's message."

"Hold on to the words, as I know you will. In time, it will come to you," the voice replied.

"Please let the Watcher know that I'm honored, and thank him for me," Isabelle said. "Now, do you know where I want to go?"

"Of course I do," the voice replied.

"By the way," Isabelle said. "Awesome eyes."

Those big blue eyes batted their eyelashes twice, followed by the right eye slowly tossing a wink at her. A huge smile lit up Isabelle's face. The Elevator door then slid closed, and we were carried away.

"Isabelle, were you able to read that message?" Sophie asked. She followed with, "The words were nothing more than a blur to me. I couldn't make out anything."

"It was clear as day," Isabelle answered. She then turned to me, asking, "How about you, Dawson? Could you make it out?"

"I was able to read the first two words, *Blood of*. Then, instantly, the rest of the message became impossible to read. All of the letters seemed to smear together into a blur. It's as if the Elevator made a quick adjustment to shut me out."

"This is strange. The Elevator must have encrypted it for my eyes only," Isabelle said. "For what reason, I'm unsure. Unless, this is how the Watcher wanted it to be."

The Elevator soon came to a stop. As the door slid open all I could see was darkness. As my eyes began to adjust I realized we were stepping out into a forest at night. Dark, ominous shadows filled the spaces between the trees in front of us, creating an eerie setting for us to pass through. I heard Sophie unholster her pistol. She must have been creeped out by the view. I know that I was.

"Are you alright, babe? Do you see something?" I asked.

"No. Just waiting for my eyes to adjust. It's a little scary out here." A moment later, I heard her return the gun to its holster. As we slowly made our way forward, I noticed a small dirt road that crossed our path about twenty yards in front of us.

Upon reaching the road, Isabelle said, "I'm finally home now, ten minutes later than when I left."

Sophie, no longer spooked by the darkness, said, "C'mon, Dawson, let's walk her home. But first," she added, as she began digging through the backpack, coming out with the two silver scarfs. "Take these, Isabelle, as something to remember us by."

Isabelle gave Sophie a hug and said, "Thank you, Sophia. I'll treasure them for lifetimes."

We walked with Isabelle along the narrow dirt road until we reached the side of her house. There, Isabelle turned to face me. With a flirtatious tone, she said, "Dawson, don't you forget about me."

"There's not a chance of that," I said with a smile.

Instantly, Isabelle's mouth dropped open, drawing in a quick breath of surprise. Her face took on an expression of wide-eyed wonder. "It just came to me. Now, I understand the message," Isabelle cried out happily.

I glanced in Sophie's direction. She seemed as puzzled as I was. "Well, what does it mean?" I asked.

Isabelle was gazing at me now with a warm loving glow. She looked as if someone had just handed her a cute little puppy. "I'm sorry, Dawson. This is how the Watcher wanted it. He granted me a gift. He opened my eyes wider, making me aware of something while you were still here. I will be forever thankful to him." Isabelle burst into tears and lunged forward, wrapping her arms around me in a big hug. "I will think about you always. I love you!" she cried.

I glanced at Sophie and saw that long sad face settling in. Her eyes welled up, spilling tears that trickled down her cheeks. She stepped closer, gently placing her hands on Isabelle's arm and shoulder. Isabelle reached back, wrapping her arm around Sophie, and pulled her in close to us. The two of them took one look at each other and the floodgates opened. The emotions were pouring out of both Isabelle and Sophie. Tears of sorrow echoed the heartache they were feeling, knowing that in the moments to follow we would become separated by hundreds of years.

Isabelle pulled her head back to look at me, face to face. With tears in her eyes she gave me a kiss, then stroked my cheek with her hand. "I can't believe that I'm younger than you right now," she said with a sniffle.

"Yeah. I know. It does seem a little odd."

"More so, than you realize. Can you do me a favor?"

"I think you already know that answer. Of course I will."

"When you get home, search deep into your past."

Isabelle next turned to face Sophie. The two of them were still spilling tears. Isabelle said, "I feel like I'm saying good-bye to my sister." Sophie hugged Isabelle tightly in return. "Don't forget what I told you," Isabelle said.

Sophie replied with a squeaky voice, "I won't. And if you happen to be around in our time, you make sure to look us up."

"That sounds like a plan," Isabelle said as she slowly backed away. With tears running down her cheeks, she said, "I will never forget the two of you and what you have done for me. I will cherish, forever, my thoughts of you. I love you both!" Isabelle wiped the tears from her eyes, smiled at us, and blew a kiss our way. She then turned the corner and headed for the front door.

I motioned to Sophie, to follow me over to the window. When she got close, I whispered softly, "I want to listen to make sure we landed in the right time, and that her family is actually in there." Sophie nodded her head in agreement.

We heard the front door open, followed by Isabelle's mother's voice. "Isabelle, thank God you're okay. Where have you been? You had me worried sick. I told you to be home before dark."

"I'm sorry, Mama. I was delayed for a while. I...I love you so much, Mama!"

"Ohh...A big hug. Thank you. I love you too, my sweet darling. My goodness...You're crying and shaking. Are you sure you're okay?"

"Yes, Mama...I am now."

With that, we quietly slipped away. Once we had reached the road, Sophie began to cry. I slipped my arm around her shoulder. "I'm so happy for her, Dawson. She found a way to return to the same age. Then return back home, only ten minutes later than when she disappeared. Her family will never have to endure the emotional distress of losing her. There will be no erasing those scars in her mind, but she will have her family and her life back again, right where she left off, all the wiser."

"Yeah. She definitely made the right choice. From this point forward, she will control her destiny," I said.

CHAPTER 45

SOPHIE'S TEARS WERE short-lived, for she knew that Isabelle was happy to be finally home again. Her thoughts now turned in a different direction. "Dawson, once the Elevator returns us to the movie theatre, we might have a problem. We're going to attract a lot of negative attention walking out with this crossbow."

"Not a problem, babe." I took the crossbow from her and held it up by the stirrup, so that it pointed upward toward the sky. "When you look at it, doesn't it resemble a big coat hanger with a tail?"

"Yeah, you're right. It does."

"If I stretch the bow's lath by pulling the string back to the lock position, I'll have plenty of room to hang my coat over it like a coat hanger. I can then carry it by the stirrup and no one will know."

"I like that idea," she said.

I stopped there for a moment, slipping the backpack off my shoulder. "And let me see if I can squeeze this bow into the bag for now, so we don't have to carry it by hand." After removing the bottle of wine from the backpack, I slid the stock of the crossbow down in next to the sword. The bow, or lath, stuck out from the top of the pack like the letter - T. I pulled the zippers snugly up against the stock to secure it. Then, I slung the backpack over my shoulder again. After picking up the bottle of wine, I eased out its cork before saying, "Alright, Sophie. This is the second time you hugged Isabelle and cried. Do you remember the first time?"

"Yeah. Of course I do."

I took a big sip of wine before handing the bottle to her. "Was it yesterday, or a hundred years from now?"

Sophie took a sip of wine while she wrestled with the question. A moment or two later she handed the bottle back to me, asking, "And is there a correct answer?"

I took one more sip before answering, "Both." Then, I pressed the cork back into the wine bottle and slid it into a side pocket of the backpack.

"I don't understand. How can it be both? How would you explain that?"

"Relativity."

After a few seconds, she said, "That's your answer, one word, relativity. You're not getting away that easy, Einstein. You have to explain your answer."

It was easy to see that she was starting to get her feathers a bit ruffled. I looked at her with a smirk on my face. "Alright. Relative to today and the people who live here, it happened a hundred years from now. But, relative to you and me, it happened yesterday." Sophie seemed to be pondering over those words for a brief moment. I playfully added, "I guess that makes me smarter than you."

"Careful, Dawson. I still have arrows."

"Ohh...That hurt," I said with a laugh. "Speaking of which, where the hell did you learn to shoot like that?"

Sophie started laughing at me as she said, "Did you forget where you met me?"

"No...I just didn't think you could shoot like that. You know what this means, don't you? Now I'll never be able to marry you. Every time we get into an argument, arrows will be flying all around me."

It was Sophie who was wearing the smirk now. "Then, just don't argue with me...And who says I'd marry you anyway?"

"You know you love me."

"Says who?"

"You said so, yesterday, today, and a hundred years from now."

A big smile came over her face as she looked upward into the night sky. "I can't find the moon tonight, Dawson."

"It's probably hidden behind the trees."

"The sky is filled with stars."

"Amatory glances," I said.

"What?"

"Every star that you see represents an amatory glance we've shared," I replied. She turned her head to me, smiling, with her eyebrows raised and a warm glow in her eye. "See. You just made another star," I said.

Sophie slipped her arm under mine and whispered, "Let's go home, Dawson."

"Are you sure ya don't want to stay here. It's so peaceful and serene. I'm sure the pace of life is much more relaxed and easygoing."

"There's also no plumbing or electricity. And I'd so miss my clothing and shoe stores."

"You also forgot, no fast food. You'd have to cook every day."

"Take me home, Dawson."

"Well, My Lady, as a matter of fact, you're in luck. We're almost to the Elevator now. I can see the spot where we came out of the woods just up ahead."

"You know...You still owe me a kiss from the first time we entered the Elevator."

I laughed inside, thinking, *There goes that elephant mind again.*

Once we reached the location we had entered from, I stopped and peered into the forest, saying, "I know this is the spot, but I don't see the Elevator anymore."

"That's because I'm standing right beside you."

The two of us did a double take, startled by the Elevator's voice coming from right next to us. Sophie jumped behind me as we both looked in the direction that the voice came from. As we watched with wide open eyes, a giant warrior suddenly materialized out of thin air. He was every bit of ten feet tall. He wore a helmet and body armor that were silver in color. His skin tone was a steel-gray, and he did indeed have those cat-like blue eyes. In his right hand, he held a weapon that resembled a tall, ornate scepter.

"I am the Herald and this is my true form of identity. We haven't much time. Your assistance is needed over here." He led us to the other side of the road, where he pointed between the trees toward the body of a young fallen soldier. "After your departure, I heard gurgling noises from across the road. He is very weak and near death. I froze him to buy some extra time while we awaited your return. You know what to do."

I looked back at the Herald, saying, "This is beyond us. He needs a team of doctors." The warrior then turned his head to look directly at Sophie.

"I know what to do," she said.

I stared at her with a puzzled face until I saw her remove from her pocket one of those small bottles of Voltaire's blood. Sophie smiled at me, saying, "Isabelle gave this to us. It's supposed to be just for you and me. But, I'm sure we could spare a couple of drops for him."

"I'm all for it. It's worth a try if it will save his life," I said.

"And in turn, your own," the warrior muttered.

"What was that?" I asked.

The Herald avoided answering my question by saying, "We must hurry. Time is of the essence." He started off the side of the road into the woods toward the fallen soldier. Sophie and I followed close behind. As we drew closer I noticed, off to my right, the torn apart bodies and remains of many other soldiers scattered and strewn about.

Upon reaching the soldier I could see that he was quite young, still in his teens. His body was very pale and showed no signs of movement. The Herald looked toward Sophie and asked, "Are you ready?"

"Yes. I am," she responded.

The Herald waved his scepter over the young man's body while Sophie applied a few drops of Voltaire's blood to the wound on his neck. A few moments later the young soldier began to make some gurgling noises and seemed to be struggling to breathe. Within only a minute or two more his body began to make some rather rapid improvements. His breathing was now smooth and rhythmic. His skin tone was returning, and that wound on his neck was mending itself back together.

Suddenly, the young soldier's eyes popped open. He looked up at the three of us with a confused expression. The giant warrior knelt down beside him and said, "Do not be alarmed. The three of us are from the future. We have been sent here to save your life. You were attacked by a band of vampires. Not to worry. They will not find you again. The day will come when they are destined to run into us, and at that point we shall vanquish all of them. We have already seen it happen."

Sophie and I looked at each other with smirks on our faces as we mouthed to each other, "We."

The Herald continued, "We were sent here by the young angel you saw earlier in the woods. I will now tell you young man, that England does not win this war. You have been granted a new life. Once you feel strong enough, make your way up the road to the first house on the left. The people there are very kind and will take you in. The young girl you refer to as an angel happens to live there. Her name is Isabelle. Mention that Dawson and Sophie saved you. She will understand. Once the two of you meet, everything else will fall into place."

The Herald stood up and turned to Sophie and me, saying, "It is time for us go. He will be fine." We followed the giant warrior back out to the road. He then asked, "Is it your wish to go home now?"

"Yes. But first, I have a question," I said.

"Proceed," said the Herald.

"Why us? Why didn't you just do this yourself? I'm sure you're capable," I said.

"I am much more than capable. But, it's not as easy as that. Yours is one of those worlds that I protect and defend from outside aggressors. The key word here is outside aggressors, for I am sworn not to take part in matters that arise between the lifeforms native to your planet."

"So, you protect our planet from other worlds?"

"The universe is full of predators and merciless conquerors. I, as well as the other heralds, protect your world by keeping you hidden, or under the radar as you might say. When predatory invaders take an interest in your planet, we intervene and take the fight to them.

"As for why the two of you, I saw in both of you the right set of skills along with a gritty courage under pressure. You seem to have a knack of finding a way to win, even when the odds are stacked against you. Sophia and Dawson, you both share a bold, persevering nature. I found myself impressed by your actions and will remain eternally grateful to you."

Out of the side of my mouth, I whispered to Sophie, "Ya know. I kinda like this guy. I'll bet he'd make a hell of a drinking buddy."

"Daw...son," she scolded under her breath. Sophie then looked up at the warrior and asked, "Can you take us home now?"

The giant warrior nodded his head, saying, "That I can." He waved his scepter in front of him and disappeared into thin air. A moment later, the Elevator reappeared. After Sophie and I stepped in, the door slid closed behind us, and the Elevator began to move.

"So, do you still want to see that movie when we get back?" I asked.

"No. Not really," Sophie answered as she stepped over closer. Facing me now, she gently slid her hands up over the top of my shoulders and locked eyes with me. Softly, she said, "We could go back to my house. I'll whip up an omelette for you while you grab some logs and get a fire going. Then, we can take that bottle of wine and snuggle up in front of the fire. How's that sound?"

"Hmmm...Let me think. I did wanna rearrange my closet," I answered jokingly.

"I had you at omelette. Didn't I?"

"Yeah ya did," I replied matter-of-factly.

A smug smile came over Sophie's face. Playfully, she whispered, "I do believe, you still owe me something."

I gazed at Sophie for a moment with just a hint of a smile, before slowly drifting closer for that kiss. However, just before our lips met, the Elevator suddenly came to an abrupt halt. Something didn't seem quite right to me. I could tell by the look on Sophie's face that she also felt something was amiss.

After a few moments of silence the Elevator spoke to us. "Forgive me. I had every intention of bringing you straight home. However, I cannot at this time, for your presence has been requested by another."